"Someone could be trying to set you up, Naomi," Devon said.

"Jessica's murder in your massage room. Your car—or at least, one similar to your car—used to run me down, maybe *another* murder."

Suddenly the threat to his own life seemed paltry compared to the insidious web being woven around her. He had to find a way to keep her safe.

She stared at him. "What can you do about it?"

What *could* he do about it? What right did he have to do anything about it?

Her chin lifted as she stood there, challenging him with her silence.

He shouldn't get involved.

But he already was involved.

At least, that's what his heart was telling him.

CAMY TANG

writes romance with a kick of wasabi. Originally from Hawaii, she worked as a biologist for nine years, but now she writes full-time. She is a staff worker for her San Jose church youth group and leads a worship team for Sunday service. She also runs the Story Sensei fiction critique service, which specializes in book doctoring. On her blog, she gives away Christian novels every Monday and Thursday, and she ponders frivolous things like dumb dogs (namely, hers), coffee-geek husbands (no resemblance to her own...), the writing journey, Asiana and anything else that comes to mind. Visit her Web site at www.camytang.com.

DEADLY INTENT
CAMY TANG

Steeple
Hill®

Published by Steeple Hill Books™

STEEPLE HILL BOOKS

Steeple
Hill®

ISBN-13: 978-0-373-44347-5

DEADLY INTENT

Copyright © 2009 by Camy Tang

Printed in U.S.A.

The Lord your God is with you,
He is mighty to save.
—*Zephaniah* 3:17

To Mom and Dad—my "publicist" and
"local bookseller."

ONE

The man who walked into Naomi's father's day spa was striking enough to start a female riot.

Dark eyes swept the room, which happened to be filled with the Sonoma spa's staff at that moment. She felt his gaze glance over her like a tingling breeze. Naomi recognized him instantly. Dr. Devon Knightley.

For a wild moment, she thought, *He's come to see me.* And her heart twirled in a riotous dance.

But only for a moment. Sure, they'd talked amiably— actually, more than amiably—at the last Zoe International fund-raising dinner, but after an entire evening sitting next to her, he hadn't asked for her phone number, hadn't asked for any contact information at all. Wasn't that a clear sign he wasn't interested?

She quashed the memory and stepped forward in her official capacity as the spa owner's daughter and acting manager. "Dr. Knightley. Welcome."

He clasped her hand with one tanned so brown that it seemed to bring the heat of the July sun into the airy, air-conditioned entranceway. "Miss Naomi Grant." His voice had more than a shot of surprise, as did his looks as he took in her pale blue linen top and capris, the same uniform as the gaggle of spa staff members gathered behind her. "It's been a few months since I've seen you."

He still held her hand. She loved the feel of his palm—cool and warm at the same time, strong the way a surgeon's should be.

No, she had to stop this. Devon and his family were hard-core atheists, and nothing good would come out of giving in to her attraction. "What brings you here?"

"I need to speak to Jessica Ortiz."

An involuntary spasm seized her throat. Of course. Glamorous client Jessica Ortiz or plain massage therapist Naomi Grant—no comparison, really.

But something in his tone didn't quite have the velvety sheen of a lover. He sounded almost…dangerous. And danger didn't belong in the spa. Their first priority was to protect the privacy of the guests.

"Er…Ms. Ortiz?" Naomi glanced at Sarah, one of the receptionists, whose brow wrinkled as she studied her computer monitor behind the receptionists' desk. Naomi knew she was stalling—she didn't need to look because she'd checked Ms. Ortiz into the elite Tamarind Lounge almost two hours before.

Naomi's aunt Becca also stood at the receptionists' desk, stepping aside from her spa hostess duties to allow Naomi to handle Dr. Knightley, but Aunt Becca's eyes had a sharp look that conveyed her message clearly to Naomi: the clients' privacy and wishes come first.

Naomi cleared her throat. "Are you her physician?"

Dr. Knightley frowned down at her, but she kept her air of calm friendliness. He grimaced and looked away. "Er…no."

Naomi blinked. He could have lied, but he hadn't. "If you'll wait here, I can see if Ms. Ortiz is available to come out here to see you." If Jessica declined to come out, Naomi didn't want to think what Devon's reaction would be.

His eyes grew stormier. "Couldn't you just let me walk in back to see her?"

"I'm sorry, but we can't allow nonfamily members into the back rooms. And men are not allowed in the women's lounges." Especially the secluded Tamarind Lounge, reserved only for Tamarind members who paid the exorbitant membership fee.

"Naomi, surely you can make an exception for me?" He suddenly flashed a smile more blinding than her receptionist's new engagement ring.

His switching tactics—from threatening to charming—annoyed her more than his argumentative attitude. She crossed her arms. "I'm afraid not." She had to glance away to harden herself against the power of that smile.

"You don't understand. It's important that I see her, and it won't take long." He leaned closer, using his height to intimidate.

He had picked the wrong woman to irritate. Maybe her frustrated attraction made her exceptionally determined to thwart him. Her jaw clenched and she couldn't help narrowing her eyes. "Joy Luck Life Spa has many high-profile clients. If we let anyone into our elite lounges, we'd lose our sterling reputation for privacy and discretion."

"You don't understand how important this is—"

"Dr. Knightley, so nice to see you again." Aunt Becca stepped forward and inserted herself between the good doctor and Naomi's line of vision. She held out a thin hand, which Devon automatically took. "Why don't I set you up in the Chervil Lounge while Naomi looks for Ms. Ortiz?"

Aunt Becca whirled around faster than a tornado. Her eyes promised trouble if Naomi didn't comply. "Naomi."

Aunt Becca's taking charge of the conversation seemed to drive home the point that although Dad had left Naomi in charge of the spa while he recovered from his stroke, she still had a long way to go toward learning good customer relations. Part of her wanted to be belligerent toward Devon just to prove she was in the right, but the other part of her wilted at her failure as a good manager.

She walked into the back rooms and paused outside the door to the Tamarind Lounge, consciously relaxing her face. Deep breath in. Gently open the door.

Softly pitched conversation drifted into silence. Two pairs of eyes flickered over her from the crimson silk chaise lounges in the far corner of the luxuriant room, but neither of them belonged to Jessica Ortiz. Vanilla spice wafted around her as she headed toward the two women, trying to glide calmly, as the daughter of the spa owner should.

"Good morning, ladies. I apologize for the intrusion."

"Is it already time for my facial?" The elderly woman gathered her Egyptian cotton robe around her and prepared to stand.

"No, not yet, Ms. Cormorand. I've come to ask if either of you have seen Ms. Ortiz."

An inscrutable look passed between them. What had Jessica done to offend these clients in only the couple of hours she'd been at the spa? Jessica seemed to be causing the spa more and more trouble recently.

The other woman finally answered, "No, she left about a half hour ago for her massage. I thought she was with you."

Naomi cleared her throat to hide her start. Jessica's appointment was at eleven, in fifteen minutes, not now.

"Yes, doesn't she always ask for you when she comes?" Ms. Cormorand blinked faded blue eyes at her.

Naomi shoved aside a brief frisson of unease. Jessica should be easy to find. "Which massage therapist called for her?"

"Oh, I don't know." Ms. Cormorand waved a pudgy hand beringed with rubies and diamonds. "Someone in a blue uniform."

Only one of almost a hundred staff workers at the spa.

"Thank you, ladies. Ms. Cormorand, Haley will call you for your facial in fifteen minutes." Naomi inclined her head and left the room, trying to let the sounds of running water from the fountain in the corner calm her growing sense of unease.

Where could Jessica have gone? And an even juicier question: Why did Devon Knightley need to speak to her?

She peeked into the larger Rosemary lounge, which was for the use of spa clients who were not Tamarind members. Several women chatted in small groups, but no Jessica Ortiz. Naomi hadn't really expected Jessica to forgo the more comfortable elite lounge, but the only other option was checking each of the treatment rooms individually.

She headed into the back area where the therapy rooms were located, navigating the hallway scattered with teak and bamboo furniture, each sporting East Asian cushions and throws, artfully arranged by Aunt Becca. Had Jessica switched to a different massage therapist? And had someone forgotten to tell Naomi in the excitement of Sarah's new engagement?

As she moved down the hallway, she started noticing a strange, harsh scent suffusing the mingled smells of sandalwood and vanilla. Not quite as harsh as chemicals, but not a familiar aromatherapy fragrance, a slightly discordant counterpoint to the spa's relaxing perfume.

She knew that smell, but couldn't place it. And it didn't conjure up pleasant associations. She started to hurry.

She first looked into the women's restroom, her steps echoing against the Italian tile. No sound of running water, but she peeked into the shower area. A few women were in the rooms with the claw-foot bathtubs, and a couple more in the whirlpool room, but no Jessica. No one using the toilets.

The mirrored makeup area had a handful of women, but again no Jessica. Naomi smiled at the clients to hide her disappointment and growing anxiety as she entered. She noticed some towels on the floor, a vase of orchids a little askew, and some lotions out of place on the marble counter running the length of the room, so she tidied up as if she had intended to do so, although the staff assigned to restroom duty typically kept things spic and span.

She peeked into the sauna. A rather loud ring of laughing women, but no Jessica.

Back out in the central fountain area, the harsh smell seemed stronger, but she couldn't pinpoint where it came from. Had a sewage pipe burst? No, it wasn't that sort of smell. It didn't smell *rotten,* just…had an edge to it.

She entered the locker area, although the Joy Luck Life Spa "lockers" were all carved teakwood cabinets, individually locked with keys. The smell jumped tenfold. Naomi scoured the room. Maybe it came from a client's locker? No. Maybe the dirty laundry hamper?

Bingo.

She flipped open the basketweave lid.

And screamed.

TWO

The scream pierced Devon's eardrums. Beside him, Becca Itoh started. The heavy wooden double doors she'd just opened, leading to the men's lounge, clunked closed again as she turned and headed back down the corridor they'd walked.

"Where—?" He kept up with her, but not easily—for a woman in her fifties, she could book it.

"The women's lounge area." She pointed ahead as she hustled closer. "Those mahogany double doors at the end."

Devon sprinted ahead and yanked open the doors. "Stay behind me."

Becca ignored him, thrusting ahead and shouting, "Naomi!" as they entered a large circular entry area with more corridors leading from it. "Naomi!"

A door to their right burst open and Naomi Grant spilled into the entry room. "Aunt Becca!" Her face was the same shade as the cream-colored walls. "There's blood in the women's locker room."

"Blood?" Becca reached for her as Devon pushed past her into the room she'd just exited.

Despite the urgency, he couldn't help but be awed by the fountain in the center of a vast chamber with a veined-tile floor. Scrollwork signs on the walls pointed to "sauna" and "whirlpool" and "locker room." Luckily, no women appeared. He veered right.

He almost wasn't sure he'd actually arrived in the right place, but the carpeted room lined with teakwood locking cabinets was in line with the luxurious entry hall of what he realized was the women's bathroom.

The metallic smell of blood reached him. He followed his nose to the basket hamper in the corner, filled with bloody towels. It reminded him of the discarded gauzes from his orthopedic surgeries, bright red and a lot more than the average person saw.

This was not good.

He returned to the two women. Naomi's hands were visibly shaking, although her voice remained low and calm. "And I couldn't find Ms. Ortiz."

Jessica's name still caused the reflexive crunching of his jaw. But he'd never wanted any harm to come to her—she wasn't a bad person, they had just clashed too much on personal matters. And now she was missing, and there was an immense amount of blood in the bathroom. Devon's heart beat in a light staccato against his throat. She had to be okay.

"Where else have you looked?" He scanned the other corridors leading from the fountain entryway. He'd need guidance or he'd get lost in this labyrinth.

"I haven't checked the therapy rooms yet." Naomi nodded toward the larger central corridor, which ended at another set of double doors.

He headed toward them when Becca reached out to grab his arm in a bony but strong grip. "You can't just barge into private sessions."

"Why not?" He turned to face the two women. "There's blood in your bathroom and Jessica Ortiz is missing."

Naomi's light brown eyes skewered him. "Do you really think it's wise to cause a panic?"

"And I suppose you have another option?"

"Sessions don't last more than an hour or ninety minutes. We'll wait for those to finish—if Jessica's just in one of those, there's nothing to worry about. In the meantime, we'll check all the empty session rooms," Naomi said.

Becca turned to leave and said over her shoulder, "I'll check on the schedule at the receptionists' desk to find out which rooms have clients and when the sessions end. I'll call you on your cell."

Naomi turned down a corridor in the opposite direction, this one lined with bamboo tables draped with shimmery, lavender-colored fabric so light that it swayed as they moved past.

It reminded Devon of the papery silks he'd seen in Thailand, giving the spa a soothing and very Asian atmosphere. His heartbeat slowed. Jessica was probably fine and had accidentally taken someone else's session in her artless, friendly way. She'd emerge from a facial or a manicure in a few minutes and wonder what all the fuss was about.

A group of three therapists turned a corner. They spied Naomi and immediately stopped chatting among themselves, although not fearfully—more out of respect that the boss was suddenly in front of them.

"Girls, have you seen Ms. Ortiz?" Naomi's smile seemed perfectly natural and warm—inviting a rapport with her staff, yet not too cozy. If Devon hadn't noticed her fingers plucking at the linen fabric of her pants, he wouldn't have known how anxious she was.

Two of them shook their heads, but the tall blond

woman to his left nodded and pointed directly across the corridor. "I saw her talking to Ms. Fischer about an hour ago before Ms. Fischer went in for her manicure."

Devon's heartbeat picked up. "An hour ago?"

The blonde eyed him with a hard look, but a quick glance at Naomi seemed to allay her suspicions. He had the impression that if her boss hadn't been by his side, he'd have been thrown out, even if it took all three women to do it.

Naomi was shaking her head. "Ms. Cormorand saw her leave the Tamarind Lounge only thirty minutes ago."

His hopes popped and fizzled.

The blonde jerked her head at the nearby door. "Ms. Fischer is almost done in room thirty-five if you want to talk to her anyway."

"That's a good idea. Thanks, Betsy."

Betsy nodded, and the silent trio headed down the corridor and around the corner.

The number thirty-five had been engraved into a brass plate that also had a small Victorian-style lantern attached, which was lit. Naomi glanced at the other doors around it. "Let's check these while we're waiting. She should be done soon."

He pushed on a half-open door to reveal a small but neat room decorated with more silks on the walls and a few low tables covered with more Thai fabric.

Aside from the facial chair and a small cabinet in the corner, the room was empty, so he withdrew.

He peeked into another room, feeling suddenly ten years old again, visiting his Aunt Gertrude in her Victorian house filled with valuables and history. The statues, the furniture, the ambience—everything screamed both decadence and privilege, similar to the Hollywood spas he'd heard of. Naomi dressed like one of the staff, but this must be an enormous business to run.

They'd finished checking all the empty rooms in the corridor when a door clicked open. Immediately, Naomi scurried to number thirty-five, where a tall woman in her late forties had just sashayed out, absently waving her pink-tipped fingers. At the sight of Devon, she carefully pinched closed the neck of her loosely tied robe, and a pulse blipped at her throat.

"Ms. Fischer, I apologize for bothering you." Naomi drew the woman's eyes from burning holes in Devon's head. "Were you speaking with Ms. Ortiz before your manicure? We're looking for her."

Ms. Fischer stiffened her shoulders and sniffed. "She was heading toward the Tamarind Lounge." Her heavy-lidded eyes drifted away from Naomi's face.

"Did she mention any of her appointments today?"

"Her massage."

"Did she mention when or with whom?"

Ms. Fischer's gaze shifted back to Naomi. "What do you mean? With you, naturally." She sniffed again.

"Thank you, Ms. Fischer. Enjoy the rest of your day at Joy Luck Life." With a professional smile, Naomi turned and headed back the way they'd come. Devon hustled to escape Ms. Fischer's disapproving glare.

Naomi turned down another corridor. "These are the massage rooms. They tend to be the busiest."

As soon as he entered the hallway he smelled it. Blood. Metallic and harsh. His chest tightened, and he grabbed Naomi's wrist to keep her from moving forward.

She fought at first, but then she smelled it, too. Her dry lips parted and she scanned the rows of doors, some open, some closed.

"Stay close." He reached out to ease open the first door, which was halfway closed. Peering in, he saw only a dark, empty massage room with the padded table draped in white linen and ready for the next client.

He didn't realize he still held her wrist until she gently disengaged it. His palm chilled as if missing her warm skin.

The next open door was on her side of the corridor. She reached out to push it more fully open, but he stopped her. "No, let me do it."

Her face seemed calm at first, but he noticed a wildness around the edges of her eyes as she peered into the darkness beyond the cracked door. "That's my massage room." Her voice was high and strangled.

Her massage room door was barely open, unlike the other doors along the corridor, which were either closed or at least halfway open to show the empty status of the room. He eased it open.

The soft light from the corridor fell on the edge of a dark pool.

His nerves fired like a popping spark plug. He grabbed Naomi's arm and shoved her against the wall. She didn't protest—she'd seen the blood.

Chattering voices suddenly tinkled from the other end of the corridor as a client in a bathrobe was escorted by a staff in uniform.

"Stop." Naomi's voice shot toward them. Her raised hand trembled. "Lavinia, please escort Ms. Everingham to the Tamarind Lounge."

Lavinia halted, mouth open, but in the next second, she turned to her client with an overwide smile. "I don't think you've ever been in the Tamarind Lounge, have you, Ms. Everingham? Follow me. It's normally reserved for

Tamarind members only, so you're in for a treat today." She continued to chatter as they turned the corner out of sight.

Now *that* was a well-trained staff. The Grants impressed him more and more.

A low moan issued from the room.

His heart pulsed hard. He pushed open the door.

Blood was everywhere. He'd seen lots of it in his surgeries, but the sight now made his throat tighten. Behind him, Naomi gagged.

A woman lay on the floor next to the massage table, and Devon's breath stopped a moment at the sight of the platinum-blond corkscrew curls. *Jessica.*

He dropped to his knees to turn her over.

She gasped a spray of blood. What looked like a blunt-force trauma injury bled from her temple.

"Towels?" he asked.

Naomi darted toward the cabinet in the corner while he looked for anything lying near him. He grabbed the sheet covering the massage table and applied pressure to her wound. Warm liquid seeped through the fabric of his pants, pooling around his kneecaps. The room had a sickening, metallic, vanilla smell.

Naomi kneeled next to him, her arms full of towels. "It's all right, Ms. Ortiz, you'll be fine."

He fumbled in his pants pocket and withdrew his cell phone, but she grabbed it from him. "Keep helping her. I'll dial 911."

"Put it on speakerphone so I can talk to the dispatcher. I'll need to talk to the trauma team."

Under the blood staining her face, Jessica's skin was paler than her hair. Half-lidded dark eyes found his.

"Andrea," she whispered.

And closed her eyes.

THREE

Naomi had never seen someone die before.

Even when her mother had died, she and her sisters had been forced to stay home with Aunt Becca while her father went to the hospital alone. Mom had been killed instantly by the drunk driver, and Dad hadn't wanted them to see her.

Aunt Becca rubbed Naomi's arms and patted her cheeks now, as she had done that night. "It's all right, Naomi."

"No, it's not all right." Naomi had to speak around her chattering teeth. She wore two of the spa bathrobes and still felt as if she'd taken an arctic swim. "Poor Jessica. I've been massaging her for years. And now she's gone." Her voice cracked.

Jessica had always been friendly, if a little ditzy. Always said something to make her laugh. Had such a sweet, airy smile when explaining why she had to stay in the room longer than she was scheduled for. Jessica had been self-centered, but pleasant about it so that Naomi almost didn't mind that her client was trying to get away with something.

"How are we going to tell Dad? This is going to make him determined to come to the spa, despite his condition."

Becca gave her a little shake. "Even though your father's a stubborn old cuss, your sister Monica is even worse than he is, under all her sweet demeanor. She won't let him do anything that would hurt himself." A twinkle appeared in her eye. "Besides, he's not cleared to drive yet, and I'm pretty sure Monica hid his car keys."

Speaking of sisters… "Where's Rachel?"

"She's still in her lab. She's in the middle of an experiment—you know how she gets—and she wouldn't be much use here, so I told her to stay."

"The detective isn't going to want to speak to her?"

"Why should he? Even though she's one of the owner's daughters, she didn't see anything because she was in the laboratory in back all morning."

And Rachel's rather spacey way of stating the bare, honest truth might get them in trouble somehow.

Aunt Becca pinched her elbow. "Calm down."

She jerked her arm away. "I am calm."

"You're as calm as a wet cat. I thought you'd bite the detective's head off earlier when he asked if the massage room was yours or not. You didn't need to tell him he could expect to find your prints all over the room in quite the tone you used."

Well, that might have been true. "He just seemed so… stern."

"But he had kind eyes." Becca smiled a bit dreamily at the thought of the detective.

Naomi didn't see Detective Carter in such a rosy light. Earlier, he'd only asked her about the massage room, but she'd been blubbering in shock, so Aunt Becca had asked him to come back later. In fact, Devon had kindly stepped in and offered to be interviewed first. Detective Carter would be interviewing her next, she was sure.

Naomi's attention was drawn to Dr. Knightley, standing with the detective near the receptionists' desk. Poor man seemed really upset—and why not? He'd come to see Jessica.

And she'd been found dying.

A shadow settled over her. Why had he needed to see Jessica so insistently? She wished she were close enough to overhear his interview with the detective.

Maybe she could arrange to get close enough.

She started making her way toward the receptionists' desk. Devon's mouth stretched tight and his words seemed clipped.

A bony hand clawed at her arm. "What are you doing?" Aunt Becca hissed.

She pulled away. "I want to know why Devon Knightley wanted to see Jessica."

"Leave them alone." Her aunt's hand clamped around her elbow this time.

Naomi turned to glare at her. "One of our clients was killed in *my* massage room. I intend to find out exactly why I found her only minutes after he appeared asking for her."

"Don't be ridiculous. Devon Knightley didn't have anything to do with it."

"How in the world would you know that?"

"I know him and I know his family. I've worked with his mother on many different charity events. Devon Knightley would never do anything so violent."

"People do unexpected things all the time in the heat of a moment."

"I know Devon Knightley. Besides, I'm a very good judge of character."

Naomi pressed her mouth closed, because she couldn't really argue when Aunt Becca's track record on who and who not to hire for the spa had been one hundred percent so far. What if she was right about Devon?

Naomi shook her head. "I can't just stand here waiting."

"You're going to get in trouble."

"I'm the acting manager of the spa. I can go wherever I please, which includes near the receptionists' desk."

Aunt Becca sighed and released her elbow. "You were never this stubborn when you were just head massage therapist."

"I didn't have to be this stubborn before Dad had a stroke and put me in charge."

With that parting shot, Naomi tried to nonchalantly make her way toward the receptionists' desk. It was a massive marble affair, but hopefully she could stand at one end and still overhear the conversation at the other end.

Detective Carter glanced her way as she approached, but she nodded professionally and then bent her head to fiddle with the appointments computer at the far end of the desk. He turned back to Dr. Knightley without hesitation, so he must not have been upset at her being nearby.

Good.

Except she couldn't hear a thing.

She stared at the computer screen intently, as if that would make her ears work better. All she could make out were a few random words: "Jessica," "talk," "known." Devon's voice was louder than the detective's, so she mostly heard his answers to questions.

How could she get closer without attracting notice?

"I didn't like her, but I didn't kill her!"

Devon's exclamation made her jump. Her hand knocked the computer mouse askew.

Which gave her an idea…

She glanced at Devon and Detective Carter, but neither seemed to notice. Devon's face had turned a motley shade of red, while the detective coolly surveyed his notebook.

She casually knocked her hand into a holder of pens and sent them scattering across the desk. Immediately she bent to pick up the one pen that fell onto the floor.

She slowly slid her hand with the pen toward her left, closer to the two men. If anyone saw her slithering along on the floor, she could show the pen as her excuse, and the pens strewn across the desk would explain the rest.

She inched her body closer to them and strained her ears. The voices sounded even more muffled because of the desk. Why hadn't she thought of that? If she got closer...

If she got *caught*...

Her heart pounded, and she closed her eyes for a brief moment. This wasn't a smart move, but she didn't care. She had to find out why Devon had so conveniently showed up, asking for a woman who was already bleeding to death in her massage room.

She crawled as quietly as she could toward the other end of the desk. Devon and Detective Carter's voices grew louder, but not just from her proximity. It sounded like tempers were rising and they couldn't keep their conversation low-pitched.

"I told you, Detective, I haven't seen her in—"

"Then how did you know she'd be here this weekend?"

A minuscule pause. "I spoke to her personal assistant and found out."

"And why did you speak to her assistant instead of Ms. Ortiz directly?"

"Jessica's impossible to talk to on the phone, and I didn't have half an hour to spare to try to keep her focused enough to answer my questions."

That sounded like Jessica. She loved rambling during her sessions, telling Naomi things she probably shouldn't know. But Jessica did that same rambling when Naomi had to settle her spa account, too, which had annoyed her.

Naomi bit the inside of her lip. It seemed wrong to remember being annoyed at her. Jessica hadn't been a bad person. Naomi had even liked her, in a way.

"Detective, you have to understand this is just a coincidence."

"And you have to understand, Dr. Knightley, that in my business, coincidences don't happen very often." The detective's voice had deepened, grown more gravelly.

"I had nothing to do with her death."

"Why did you need to speak to her now?"

"My sister's wedding is in six weeks."

"Why didn't you try to contact Ms. Ortiz before this?"

"I did, but she wouldn't take my calls."

"And so you decided to force a confrontation in a public place."

"I hoped she would be reasonable in public."

"Any particular reason you picked this place?"

"I thought she'd be in a better mood here. She's always happy to come here."

"But she's not happy, Dr. Knightley. She's dead. Your ex-wife is dead."

"What do you mean, you knew?" Naomi stared at her aunt as they stood on the other side of the foyer.

"Of course, I knew. I wouldn't be a very good hostess if I didn't know things about my clients' personal lives."

"Why would you need to know that?"

Aunt Becca gave her a hard stare. "Think about it. I might stick two mortal enemies in sessions at the same time so they'd meet in the common lounge, or in session rooms next to each other. The spa prides itself on giving high-profile clients a relaxing experience. Meeting some-one you don't like is not a relaxing experience."

"But knowing things like that… Isn't that gossip?" She had a hard time believing her religious aunt would stoop to something like that.

"It's not gossip. I get my information from the clients themselves or the people involved."

As acting manager, maybe Naomi ought to know these things as well. "Am I the only one who didn't know he's her ex-husband?"

"No, I doubt it's common knowledge. I found out from Devon's mother at a charity event we attended together last year."

"How long have they been divorced?"

"At least two years. Before Jessica started coming to our spa."

"Ahem."

Detective Carter stood in front of her. Her heart slammed into gear like a revving truck engine.

"Miss Grant, could I speak to you alone?"

Naomi glanced at Aunt Becca, but her darling aunt, the woman who had protected and raised her since Mom died, threw her to the wolves. "Why certainly, Detective. I'll just be over there." Aunt Becca pointed to the receptionists' desk several yards away. And then she was gone.

Could the detective smell fear? His "kind eyes" pene-trated her sharply. Did he know she'd overhead part of his conversation with Dr. Knightley? His penetrating gaze made her struggle not to look away guiltily.

"Your father is the owner of this spa, but where is he?"

"At home, recovering from a small stroke he suffered a few months ago."

"By himself?"

"My younger sister, Monica, is a registered nurse, and she left her hospital in San José to come home to nurse him." And wasn't too happy about it, either, but Naomi had to give Monica credit for making the sacrifice.

"Your mother is…?"

"She passed away when I was in junior high school."

"I'm truly sorry."

His sympathy made her blink harder. Mom's death still felt like pinpricks in her heart, and Jessica's death revived the old ache. She missed her mother's murmuring endearments to her in Japanese, softly so Dad wouldn't hear and complain he couldn't understand.

"Do you have any other siblings?"

"My older sister, Rachel, is a dermatologist who does research in a laboratory facility built into the back of the spa. She develops the skin treatments we use. She was in her lab all morning and didn't know about any of this, so we didn't ask her to come out here. Did you need to see her?"

"Probably not." He consulted his notes. "So Ms. Ortiz was a regular client of yours?"

"Yes, she came to the spa every few months. Her last visit was about four months ago."

"Your staff mentioned that she always requested you for her massage."

The way he said it was almost as if he'd caught her in a deliberate omission. "Yes, that's correct."

"You were with Dr. Knightley when you found Ms. Ortiz?"

"Yes." Images of poor Jessica, weak and dying, made her press her lips together.

"Describe what happened for me."

She told him in a low voice. She didn't really want to go over it again.

"You mentioned that the massage room is yours. Do all the objects inside the room belong to the spa, or are some of them your personal items?"

"Well, yes. I have my own aromatherapy oils, some knickknacks—"

"A bear statue?"

The way he said it made her start to shiver again. "Yes, a teddy bear statue. It was a birthday present from Aunt Becca."

"It's larger and heavier than most of the other statues in the room."

"It was a special commission from the artist who did the small stone statues in all the rooms—he usually does larger pieces. The teddy bear one was very expensive."

The detective stared at his notebook, but she got the impression he wasn't really reading it. His eyes lifted to hers. "The statue has a lot of fingerprints on it, Miss Grant."

"I…I touch it all the time." Her breath came in gasps. "It has that big round tummy. I rub it all the time. Because it's cute."

Detective Carter looked like the word *cute* wasn't even in his vocabulary.

Her heart grew heavy. "Are you saying it was…the murder weapon? My teddy bear statue?"

Her statue. Her room. Her client.

Naomi pressed her hand to her mouth, only then aware of how badly she was shaking. She pressed the other hand to her stomach, to stop the roiling there.

"Several of your staff members mentioned that you had an argument with Ms. Ortiz this morning?" The detective's mild tone had an edge to it.

"Not an argument," she said hastily. "She… The last time she was here, her credit card had been declined. She gave us a second one, and that was fine. But because of that, this time I asked her to run her card through before her treatment." She'd thought she was being a good manager-in-training and that Dad would be proud of her for her initiative. "Jessica wasn't upset, really, more like… confused. She has a lighthearted way of saying things that makes you think it's not a big deal."

She'd just referred to Jessica in the present tense. The thought made her nose stuff up and a tremor run across her bottom lip. "She gave us her card and it went through fine. Everything was resolved." Her voice broke on the last word.

The detective's neutral expression gave nothing away, but Naomi thought she sensed a coolness in his manner. Why didn't he believe her?

"Did you have any other problems with Ms. Ortiz?"

"No, not at all." True, Jessica had always been a bit demanding and self-centered, but always so sweet-natured about it, even when Naomi told her no.

The detective paused a long moment. Could he read her not-quite-kind thoughts about Jessica? Naomi folded her hands in front of her to prevent herself from fidgeting. She swallowed. When would this be over?

"Can you think of any reason why someone would want to hurt Ms. Ortiz?"

She shook her head. "Jessica is—was so nice." She took a deep breath. *Calm down.* "She was gorgeous, and that made some clients jealous of her." She remembered Ms. Cormorand and Ms. Fischer. "And she talked a lot about herself, so that annoyed a few clients. But nothing that would make someone want to kill her."

Detective Carter nodded as he took notes in his notebook. "I'll speak to Ms. Itoh now. I might have more questions for you later. You also might not want to leave Sonoma anytime soon."

This wasn't happening to her. This couldn't be happening. Jessica dead and herself a suspect! She couldn't breathe. She was going to faint. No, she shouldn't faint—she wouldn't.

Naomi beckoned to Aunt Becca, who walked over. The detective hadn't mentioned wanting to speak to her aunt alone, but Naomi backed up a few steps, enough to give them the semblance of privacy.

The detective turned to Aunt Becca. "Ms. Itoh—"

"Call me Becca, Detective," she said, smiling.

He smiled back—faintly, responding to her charm, but not unreservedly. He consulted his notes. "You are a hostess for the spa?"

"Yes. We have two receptionists for here in the lobby area—" she nodded toward Sarah and Iona, who stood wide-eyed and stiff against the far wall "—but for the entire back area of the spa, I am general hostess to see to the clients' needs."

"And you're also related to the Grants?"

"I'm their mother's sister. I came to live with them after she died many years ago. It's been so wonderful to raise my nieces. But I think sometimes Augustus is a little over-whelmed by having four women in the house."

Aunt Becca must have been more nervous than she let on, because she was certainly running off at the mouth. The detective's soft gray eyes seemed to smile at Aunt Becca's rambling, but they were probing at the same time.

"Miss Grant?" a nervous voice whispered.

Naomi turned. Sarah and Iona stood at her shoulder, hunched over as if that would make the detective notice them less. "Yes?" she whispered back.

Iona cast a glance at Detective Carter. "Sarah and I were talking… We caught a glimpse of Ms. Ortiz when… well, when you first found her and before the police came. And we were both just noticing—"

"It's so strange," Sarah said, nodding. "We figured you wouldn't mind if we mentioned it."

"Mentioned what?" Naomi asked.

"Well, when Ms. Ortiz came in this morning, we both noticed her necklace." Iona's voice, already low-pitched, dropped even lower. "And when we saw her—you know, in the massage room—she wasn't wearing it."

"What necklace?" Detective Carter asked.

Iona started and Sarah turned pale as the detective's eyes turned on them. Iona licked her lips. "Well…it might not be anything…"

Sarah shrugged. "It might just be in her locker, because who wears jewelry when they get a massage?"

"But we noticed she didn't have on her Tiffany diamond necklace."

"Did Ms. Ortiz have a locker?"

"Yes." Aunt Becca dipped a hand into her silk pants pocket. "I have the master key. Sarah, will you find out Ms. Ortiz's locker number on the computer, please?"

Sarah was off in a flash, her slender heels clicking smartly on the lobby's tile floor as she headed to the receptionists' desk. She hustled back with a breathless, "Number twenty-one."

Naomi led the way back toward the women's locker room, stepping under the yellow police tape, and Aunt Becca gave the key to Detective Carter. He opened cabinet twenty-one, and all three of them peeked inside.

There was a cream suit that looked expensive, hanging from the clothes bar. Salvatore Ferragamo shoes casually tossed on the floor. A minuscule Chanel clutch purse.

The detective rummaged in the purse but shook his head. No necklace. "We need to search the other lockers." He raised eyes that were no longer soft gray, but steely.

Naomi glanced at Aunt Becca.

"I'm sorry, Detective, but we'll need to insist on a warrant." Aunt Becca's voice was low but firm.

His mouth tightened. "You do realize we're trying to solve a murder." While his tone remained light and slightly gravelly, there was a frustrated edge to his words.

Aunt Becca licked her lips. "I do realize that, Detective, but you also have to realize that clients come to the Joy Luck Life Spa specifically for privacy and anonymity. We had a starlet in room thirty, a movie producer in room forty-five, and the CEO of a Fortune 500 company in room twelve."

The detective's cheek twitched, but otherwise he didn't react to the impressive list.

"If we allowed you to search the lockers without a warrant, we'd lose our reputation and our clients. I'm afraid I must stand firm on this, sir." Aunt Becca's eyes narrowed at the same moment Detective Carter's did, and they glared at each other with similar bulldog expressions. It was almost comical. Except for the fact he was a policeman.

Naomi's stomach lurched. How could Aunt Becca have the backbone to stand up to him?

Detective Carter's expression faded slowly. He straightened. "I'll be back with that warrant, Ms. Itoh." His low voice made it sound like a threat.

Aunt Becca nodded and gave a faint smile. "You do that."

Naomi's stomach didn't settle, even when the detective followed them out of the locker room. They had to do this to protect the spa, but were they allowing the murderer to go free?

FOUR

Devon had already checked into his hotel in downtown Sonoma when he noticed that his cell phone was missing.

That alarmed him more than usual, simply because it had been such a bad day.

Where had he last used it? He didn't remember using it any time today. He hadn't called his sister or his admin, who had the day off since he wasn't taking appointments today.

He didn't remember dialing anyone for any reason. He'd avoided calling his sister to tell her what happened. Rayna disliked Jessica with a passion, but the news would still shock her. Plus, Jessica's death meant it would be next to impossible to recover their mother's Tiffany necklace now. It was probably lost somewhere in Jessica's apartment, and he'd certainly never be able to show up and look for it.

He reined in his mercenary thoughts. Jessica was dead, and he could only think about his mother's necklace? Maybe the years since their divorce had made him harder than he thought.

But today, seeing Naomi Grant again, something inside him had shifted...

For the past three years at the annual Zoe International dinner, he'd enjoyed talking with Naomi. He'd actually spent too much time talking with her. But the first time he'd met her, he was going through the divorce, and the other two times, he'd been trying to rebuild his business and finances. He hadn't acted on his attraction because he'd been too distracted by other things. Plus, Naomi's personality reminded him too much of Jessica's—both bouncy and cheerful, although he sensed that Naomi had a more serious, responsible core.

Or maybe he just didn't want Naomi to be too much like Jessica.

Logically, he knew that Naomi Grant was not Jessica Ortiz. Jessica's family did have something in common with Naomi's—they were both local but successful business owners. The Ortizes owned an exclusive clothing boutique with only one physical store in San Francisco, adding to the clothing's appeal, allure and prices. Jessica had worked for her family, just as Naomi did—she'd been public relations manager for the store until she married him.

And then it had all changed.

She had spent all his money. Started running up huge bills and charging on credit.

And it was usually jewelry. Always jewelry.

And then came the divorce, when she'd taken him for everything that wasn't nailed down.

Two years later, and he was finally starting to rebuild his finances. Luckily, his reputation hadn't suffered; he'd continued to have a steady stream of patients in addition to his work with the Oakland Raiders.

He'd vowed he wouldn't be betrayed by a woman again. It wasn't just the money—he'd truly loved Jessica for several years. But her personality had changed, and she'd hurt him in ways he hadn't even admitted to his therapist.

The ugly divorce had made him more bitter toward her than he realized. Yesterday, when he'd found out from her personal secretary that she had an appointment at the Joy Luck Life Spa in Sonoma, he'd felt a sour anger that she could blithely go on with her life after ruining his.

No. He had to stop thinking about the divorce and focus on his cell phone. Naturally Jessica would be in his thoughts after what happened to her today, and he'd done all he could to help her….

Wait a minute. He *had* used his phone. Or specifically, Naomi Grant had used it to call the police. The dispatcher had put him through to the paramedics on their way so he could brief them before they arrived. And all the while, he'd been trying to stop the bleeding…but they'd been too late. She'd lost too much blood.

Jessica was gone before the paramedics arrived only minutes later.

Witness to it all, Naomi was dangerously pale, and he'd forced her out of the room.

He'd never retrieved his phone. There hadn't been time. He'd spoken more to the paramedics as they tried to save Jessica. When they finally called the time of death, he'd left the room, but Naomi was gone.

He grabbed the hotel phone and called his cell. No answer. He called the spa, but again, no answer. Well, it was nine o'clock—the spa was probably empty except for the security guards left on the premises to monitor Dr. Rachel Grant's research labs built into the backside of the spa building. He remembered Becca Itoh telling him about them a few years ago when he first met the Grants.

Wait, Becca would be able to help him. She liked him—or at least, she did before it seemed as if he were mixed up in his ex-wife's murder.

He had her business card somewhere… No, he had her private number in his cell phone. But Martha would have that number, too. He called his admin.

"Have you forgotten you gave me the day off?" No hello. Typical Martha.

"Hello to you, too. Would you please get me the private number for Becca Itoh. I-t-o-h."

"You're assuming I have my computer with me."

"You always have your computer with you. Don't think I don't know about the eBay stuff you do."

She hmphed, but he also heard the clicking of computer keys. She rattled off the number and he copied it onto a piece of paper.

"Are you going to tell me why you needed me to look it up instead of dialing it yourself on your cell phone?"

"Where's the fun in that?"

"You lost it, didn't you?"

"There were extenuating circumstances. Speaking of which, something has come up and I have to stay in Sonoma for a few days longer." Hopefully not in a jail cell. Just the thought made his stomach coil tighter.

"A few days? How many days?"

"You'll need to clear my schedule for the next week."

"The next week?" Her screech made the telephone vibrate.

"Martha, it has to do with Jessica."

She immediately quieted. "I'm sorry. That woman has caused you more hurt and headache—"

"She's dead. Murdered."

"What?"

"And I'm the prime suspect."

Silence.

"Martha?"

"This is awful. Just awful. Oh, God…"

"Your God isn't going to help me now." Why should He? He hadn't done anything about the torrential divorce, what Jessica had done to his finances, what she'd nearly done to his reputation.

Martha didn't *tsk,* but he heard it in her voice. "You're not in a position to thumb your nose at Him."

She was right. "Well, right now I need to recover my cell phone. I'll keep you posted about how long I need to stay in Sonoma."

"I'll be praying for you, Devon."

Her soft voice made the worry in his gut boil harder. "Pray I get my phone soon. Bye."

He called his cell phone again, and the spa again, both with no answer, again. Then he dialed Becca Itoh.

"Dr. Knightley. What can I do for you?"

"I'm sorry to bother you, Becca, but I think Naomi has my cell phone."

"Your cell phone?"

"She used it to call 911 earlier today."

A brief pause. "Oh."

"I called my cell and the spa, but there's no answer. Is she with you?"

"No, she's not home yet."

"Not home?" It was full dark. And Jessica had been murdered in Naomi's massage room. The killer was still out there…

"She was determined to take a late client at the spa tonight."

"I thought the spa was closed."

"We canceled all our other appointments, but Penelope Olson asked for a special session and Naomi agreed."

"I realize she's the senator's wife, but isn't it dangerous for Naomi to be there so late?"

"Don't worry, we hired an extra night guard at the spa, and they're looking out for her. I know she's still there, and you're in the Cronby Hotel, right?"

"Yes."

"You can get there in only a few minutes. She should be finishing her session in about forty minutes, so why not meet her out at the spa to get your phone? I'll call the security desk to let them know you're on your way."

"Thanks, Becca."

"In exchange, you can follow her home to make sure she's okay."

She trusted him? When he'd shown up asking for his ex-wife?

She must have read his mind. "I trust you, Devon. I know you and your family. And I think God brought you here for a reason."

God again. How odd for Him to be mentioned by both Martha and Becca, the only two women he knew who were such strong religious types.

But Becca's trust made his heart feel lighter as he hung up.

"Thanks so much for taking me, dahling," Penelope Olson cooed over her shoulder as she followed the security guard out the front door.

Naomi leaned against the receptionists' desk, but jumped when the main phone line rang. Caller ID told her it wasn't a client. "Hi, Dad."

"I just heard you're still at the spa. Why did you agree

to Penelope's special appointment after everything that's happened today?"

"Well, we had to cancel all our other appointments today and Penelope didn't know—"

"Is she still there?"

"Martin's walking her out to her car, then he'll come back to walk me to mine."

"Good. You're being safe anyway. I tried calling your cell phone but you didn't pick up."

She patted down her cotton uniform. "It must still be in my office." She always emptied her pockets before taking a client.

"Did the police come back?"

"Yes, they came back this afternoon with a warrant to search everything. But I'm not sure what they found. They didn't tell us."

"I wish Jessica Ortiz hadn't always asked for you whenever she came in," her father said.

"There's nothing suspicious in that, Dad. Lots of people are loyal to their favorite massage therapists."

"Still…the police took the videotapes from the outside cameras, right?"

"They took those this morning." In fact, Detective Carter had seemed a little annoyed that Joy Luck Life had such extensive outside video coverage and absolutely no inside coverage of the treatment and lounge areas. But he seemed to grudgingly calm down when Becca reminded him of the bankrolls of the spa's clientele, and how those bankrolls paid for the privacy of the spa.

The door swung open.

"Martin's here, Dad, I'll be home soon." She hung up.

Except it wasn't Martin, her security guard. It was a stranger.

* * *

Devon drove from downtown Sonoma out to the spa, which stood in the middle of a vineyard deeper in the valley. It was too isolated. What was Naomi thinking to stay late at the spa alone?

There were two cars in the parking lot, one of them a very nice convertible. Was one of them Naomi's car? Wouldn't she park in the employee parking lot next to the valet parking?

As he eased into a stall, one of the cars—not the convertible—came to life and backed out. The security guard—visible in the summer dusk—waved at the driver as the car pulled away, then came to Devon's vehicle.

"Good evening, sir." Respectful but firm. "The spa is closed."

"Naomi Grant has my cell phone and I need to get it back from her."

The guard frowned. "Miss Grant didn't mention you'd be coming by."

"Becca Itoh told me she'd be here."

"Ms. Itoh didn't mention it to me, either."

"If I could just speak to Naomi—"

"I'm afraid I can't let you into the spa, sir. Especially in light of what happened today."

"But I need my phone."

"Did you try calling your cell phone, sir?"

He knew the guard had to do his job, but Devon's temper started to sizzle. "Naomi isn't picking up. That's why I called Becca, who told me she was here." She'd also neglected to tell the security guards he'd be coming. What could he do? "Here's an option. Why don't you escort me to the front door and let me speak to Naomi? Besides, I'm sure you don't want to leave her alone in the spa while you're out here talking with me."

The guard stiffened and leaned back on his heels. "Miss Grant is perfectly safe, sir."

"I'm sure she is—"

"In fact, there are extra security guards at the spa tonight." The way he said it was almost like a dog growling, hackles raised.

"Well, that's good, but I—"

"And none of us received a call from Ms. Itoh about you stopping by."

"Um…you could call Ms. Itoh to verify that I'm supposed to be here."

The guard seemed torn between leaving Devon out here alone and escorting a potentially dangerous man into the spa.

"I realize that you're very protective of Naomi Grant, but I promise, all I want is my phone back. Becca Itoh will verify my story."

The guard reluctantly stepped aside to let Devon out of his car, but he kept a wary distance.

The walk from the parking lot to the front door seemed very long. Then again, the last time he'd been here, he'd pulled up at the valet station, not in the parking lot.

"Hey!" Naomi's raised voice drifted toward them from the spa entrance.

"We're closed, sir." Naomi's shoulder blades snapped back and a river of steel ran down her spine. She tried to appear calm and professional, but she found it hard to breathe with her heart galloping so fast.

The stranger wasn't even looking at her, instead darting his light eyes around the entry foyer. "I'm…uh…looking for someone."

Was he on drugs or something? He was more nervous than a cat. "There's no one else—er, I mean…" *You just told him you're by yourself!*

Where was Martin? Would he be back soon? Her eyes drifted to the seats behind the receptionists' desk and the emergency call button that would bring the other security guard to the entry foyer. She started slowly easing behind the counter.

The soft light from the lamps gleamed in his straight blond hair as he whipped his head around to look at her. "No one else? What about Jessica Ortiz?"

"Jessica Ortiz?" Her heart rammed up her throat and pulsed just below her jaw.

His light eyes turned wary. "Yes. Where is she?"

At the morgue. Except she couldn't tell him that. "Who are you?"

"I'm Jessica's friend." He had gone back to casting his gaze uneasily around the room.

Only a few more feet before she could hit the call button. "What's your name?" Detective Carter was going to love her for discovering this lead. If he didn't continue to hold *her* as the prime suspect.

The man suddenly moved around the receptionists' desk—the other side, blocking the call button—to close in on her. "Look, Jessica's not here, so where is she?"

The man had several inches on her, but it seemed like several feet. *Pull yourself together.* He had a light build. She could put up a good fight and she might even win, since she had so much upper body strength from giving massages.

Where was Martin? she wondered.

"Where *is* she?" The stranger grabbed her upper arm with slender but strong fingers.

She tried to yank away, but his fingers bit into her muscle. "Let go of me."

"I need to find her. Where is she?"

"I, uh…I don't know." Which was true, she didn't know where the morgue was.

"You're lying to me." The strange intensity of his eyes gripped her harder than his hand.

"I'm not." She jerked hard to try to break his hold.

He only stepped closer toward her.

"My security guard is coming back any moment." She hoped. "Let go of me."

He suddenly did, and she stumbled backward.

He had an inscrutable look on his face. "Something has happened to her." It wasn't a question.

Her heart had begun to slow now that he'd released her. "Do you…do you want to leave a message for her?" It was a last-ditch effort—she had to find out who he was.

He looked straight into her eyes, then he bolted.

"Hey!"

It was only then that Devon noticed the dark figure passing through the double doors of the spa, running straight toward them.

The guard stepped forward and reached for his flashlight. "You there—!"

But the unknown man barreled into the guard, knocking the flashlight away. He pinballed toward Devon.

Devon grabbed the man by his torso. The stranger had a light build but solid muscle under his cotton shirt. Devon grunted as he tried to stop him from running away. The security guard attempted to capture a flailing arm.

The man knocked the back of his elbow into Devon's throat, then smashed something into Devon's hand. It cracked and sliced into him, and his hold loosened enough for the man to burst free. The guard tripped and fell to the ground as the man sprinted away.

Devon raced after him, but the blow to his throat made it hard to breathe. The man leaped into the convertible and it roared to life as Devon reached out to touch the hood. With a squeal of tires and the heavy scent of burning rubber, the man was gone.

Then he realized. Naomi had been in the spa alone.

"Hey!"

Naomi rounded the other corner of the receptionists' desk the same time the stranger did. She ran at him, but he sidestepped and swung his arm wide, knocking her to the floor. Her elbow and chin hit the cold marble painfully.

Martin's voice filtered through the slowly closing double doors. "You there—!" Thank goodness, maybe Martin would stop the guy. She hadn't even gotten his name!

Naomi hauled open the spa's double doors in time to hear an engine roar, then fade as the car drove away. Scanning past the rose trees, she lifted on tiptoe but couldn't see the parking lot from the doorway, so she stepped outside. Then she saw Martin with Devon Knightley.

"What are you doing here? And what happened?" She opened the doors and walked back into the entrance foyer, although part of her wondered if it were safe, even with Martin there. After all, Devon was Jessica's ex-husband and he'd shown up very conveniently this morning.

Then she realized that he was injured. He wasn't dripping blood, but scarlet lanced across the back of his hand.

"Are you all right? Did that man get away?"

Martin nodded. "Sorry, Ms. Grant."

"You didn't see him when you walked Ms. Olson to her car?"

He shook his head. "He might have taken another pathway from the parking lot to the front door."

Jared, the other security guard, then rushed into the entrance foyer. "Miss Grant, are you all right?"

"Where were you?" Martin demanded.

"I'm sorry, Miss Grant, I was doing the walk-through rounds of the labs, so I wasn't in the security room to see that guy on the outside camera when he came in. When I got back to the room, I saw him when he ran out. Are you all right?"

"I'm fine, but Devon…" She motioned him to follow her back into the therapy area. Each room had a first aid kit. "Let me get you something for that. Why are you here?"

"You have my cell phone."

"I do?" Then she remembered dialing 911. She'd held the phone for him as he'd tried to…save Jessica. She must have slipped it into her pocket and then blindly thrown it on her desk before Penelope's appointment. "It's in my office. I have a first aid kit in there, too."

She hesitated. Was that wise, taking this man into her office? A part of her said, *You're being silly, this is Devon Knightley.* But the other part of her, the part that had recoiled at the sight of Jessica Ortiz bleeding on her massage room floor, told her, *He's her ex-husband, and he came in asking for her.*

Martin's eyes flickered over hers. "Ah…I'll do the routine walk-through of the therapy rooms right now, just in case."

Bless him. There was no "routine walk-through" of the

therapy rooms—only the labs in the secure area in back—so Martin would be within shouting distance. "Jared, could you please call the police for me?"

"No problem, Miss Grant."

She headed to her office, where she passed him a pink napkin, from a Victorian tea shop in San José that she had visited last weekend, to use to stop his bleeding.

He seemed almost embarrassed to look up at her, but he was smiling as he dabbed his hand with the napkin. "You treat me like a normal person rather than as the official orthopedic surgeon of the Oakland Raiders. You've always done that."

"Oh." His vulnerability warmed her. She busied herself getting the first aid kit out of a cabinet. "I guess you do get your share of fawning, same as we do."

"Because of the spa?"

"Because of Dad's money and the spa." Naomi pulled out some alcohol wipes, antibacterial ointment and some elastic bandages. "How badly are you cut?"

"Those bandages will be fine." He took the alcohol wipes from her. "Men target you and your sisters?"

"Monica seems to attract handsome-but-out-of-work actors. In fact, when she started working at that hospital in San José, I think she kept secret her ties to Joy Luck Life."

"I don't blame her. But people seem to find out somehow." He winced as he cleaned his cuts with an alcohol wipe.

"I don't know how that happens. Rachel hardly gets out at all, but some biochemist found out about her and pursued her. Rachel rarely gets mad, but she lit into him like a harpy when she discovered he was trying to see her research."

"And yourself?" He glanced up at her, pausing as he tore open an elastic bandage.

"The men I meet always seem so nice at first, but then that 'I want something from you' message always seems to seep out." If only it still didn't pierce so deep. "Dad gets the same with women."

Devon grunted in agreement as he applied ointment to the bandage and placed it over a deep cut.

Now why had she mentioned all that? She had slipped back into their easy conversation as if the events of this morning hadn't happened.

Except she had taken Devon's attention more seriously than she knew she ought to. She'd sat next to him at three Zoe charity dinners, and after each dinner, she'd spent a few weeks hoping he would contact her again. And he never had. A sigh escaped her.

He looked up at her, his dark eyes turning to onyx in the light, as if he could read her thoughts. "Not all of them want something from you."

"What?"

"Those men. They could be wanting to talk to you because you're witty and interesting."

She suddenly couldn't breathe.

He didn't look away, as if there were something in her that he liked looking at. Almost…admiration. Captivation.

Then he blinked rapidly and looked away.

Air rushed back into her lungs, and she took a deep breath. What had happened? Had that really happened?

He was busying himself with his bandages. She felt silly, sitting there watching him. Hoping he'd look up at her again. Hoping he'd look at her that way again.

Now *that* was silly. He'd probably been thinking about something else entirely.

She cleared her throat. "You never told me exactly why you needed to speak to Jessica this morning."

He paused for a moment—short enough that she wondered if she'd imagined it.

He smiled at her, but it was inappropriate, considering her question. And the smile never reached his eyes. "She was my ex-wife. There were some things we needed to discuss. Things to do with the divorce."

Naomi was tempted to pry further, but that would be too rude, especially if those things had to do with financial matters. But a niggling in her head told her he wasn't being entirely forthright with her. Why would he be evasive? What could he be hiding? This uncomfortable feeling in her gut, combined with Devon's timing this morning, was not a good sign.

But this was Devon Knightley. She'd spoken to him—for hours, at each Zoe dinner. He couldn't be involved in this nasty business, could he?

She didn't *want* him to be involved in this. That was the bare, honest truth.

He finished bandaging his hand. "Did I tell you that my sister's getting married in a few weeks?"

She reluctantly followed his change of topic. They chatted about his sister's upcoming wedding and other inconsequential things—but the conversation never returned to that same comfortable footing.

It only took twenty minutes for Detective Carter to arrive. He'd happened to be nearby when the call came through.

He seemed a bit tired to be back at the spa for the third time that day, but he did say, "Miss Grant, pretty soon you'll qualify for police frequent visitor points."

He seemed very interested in the man who'd come into the spa looking for Jessica when Naomi gave her statement. As she left so Detective Carter could interview

Devon privately in her office, she noticed the detective eyeing the garish pink napkin, still on Devon's hand.

Devon hastily threw it away in Naomi's wastebasket.

She walked down the hallway, but hesitated just within hearing range.

"Dr. Knightley, what did the man hit you with?"

"I think a pair of sunglasses. They broke against my hand, but there were no embedded glass or plastic shards, as far as I can tell."

"Where did this happen?"

"Outside. I think the pieces are still on the sidewalk."

"I'll bag it. Did you want me to call an ambulance?"

"For this? No, thanks."

Devon told the detective about his lost cell phone—which Naomi had also explained—but also about how Aunt Becca had told him to come to the spa to find her. She understood the need for him to get his phone back, but her aunt seemed to have been trusting Devon Knightley a bit too much.

Naomi called Martin in the security office to bring the outside video footage with him. He appeared and handed the video over, and then gave his statement to the detective in Naomi's office.

After he was done, he paused a moment in the doorway, glancing first at the detective, then at Devon, and lastly at Naomi.

"Did you need to tell me anything else?" Detective Carter asked him.

"No, no." He left to return to his station in the security office.

Had he wanted to say something to her, but couldn't because Devon and the detective were here? Naomi ought to talk to him tomorrow to make sure it wasn't anything important.

As the detective left, her cell phone rang. "Oh no! I didn't call Dad back to tell him why I'm not home yet. Hello?"

"What's going on?" His raised voice shot out of the phone. "I'm worried sick, here—"

"Sorry, Dad, something came up."

"Are you okay?" Dad asked.

"I'm fine. Martin and Jared were here, and Devon's here with me, too."

"Devon Knightley? Why is he there?"

"I had his cell phone—"

"So you let him into the spa at this hour? The man who showed up just when you found the *dying woman?*"

Devon's smile shifted to a pained expression, and a faint dimple appeared in one cheek. She'd never noticed it before…wait a minute, could he hear her father? "If you want to complain, talk to Aunt Becca. She's the one who told him to drive out to the spa to find me."

"Oh." Dad's voice dropped to normal decibels again. "Well, come home right now."

"Yes, sir." She ended the call.

"Naomi." Devon's voice, strong and low, planted her to the ground as effectively as the serious glint in his eyes. "I know it looks suspicious. But I didn't kill Jessica." He looked as if he needed her to believe him somehow.

"I…" What could she say? "It's hard."

His mouth tightened as he turned away for a second. "I know. But why would I deliberately ask for a woman I'd just killed?"

He had a point. She'd have found Jessica within a few minutes anyway, since the dying woman was in her massage room.

"Besides, the detective will see from the video surveillance that I never entered the building before walking in to ask for her."

Well, that made her feel stupid. She looked down at her twined hands.

"How do I know *you* didn't kill her?" Devon asked.

"What? Why would I kill her? Doing it in my own massage room?"

"It would make it look like you're being framed."

"Bringing down bad publicity on my own spa?"

Devon smiled. "Look, we're both suspects even though I didn't have the means and you didn't have a motive. Why don't we just call a truce?" He held out his hand.

He was right. "Sure."

His touch to her skin felt like a sunburn. A very pleasurable sunburn. *You idiot, it's a handshake, not a lover's caress. You're so pathetic.* She snatched her hand away. "I'll see you." She headed toward the exit doors, intent on escaping his presence even though she still had to face her father's wrath at home.

How horrible today had been. In comparison, tomorrow would be a quiet day.

FIVE

The silence of the empty spa frightened Naomi.

It hadn't been so bad this morning and afternoon as she'd taken advantage of the empty spa to catch up on paperwork. But now, she missed the sound of soft, slippered feet along the halls, the quiet conversation, even the soothing Asian-inspired instrumental music that normally piped down the halls from the sound system. The absolute quiet hung thick and suffocating. And, as the sun set, that mute cloud seemed dark and forbidding, too.

She was imagining things. She was just jittery after everything that had happened yesterday. And what a day it had been.

Her office phone rang, and she jumped. She picked up the phone. Hopefully the caller wouldn't hear her heart pounding against her throat. "Hello?"

"Miss Grant? It's David from the security desk. I just wanted to tell you that me and Ron are about to switch off with Lester and Neal for the evening shift."

"Thanks." For once, she didn't object to the extra security her father had hired for the next few days.

Poor Martin. She wished he were here instead of these other security guys. But after his full day of Jessica's tragedy in the morning and then staying late only to run into that stranger, he deserved the next few days off.

She only had a stack of job applications to go through now—and she really needed to do it, because Sarah had given her two-week notice—but the sight oppressed her. How could this be happening to the spa? Only two days ago, they'd been thriving enough to need to hire more therapists and aestheticians, and today, they might need to let some personnel go if Jessica's murder sullied the spa's reputation in the next month or so.

She shouldn't be thinking of something so mundane, not when a woman had lost her life. And in her spa room. But because Jessica had been her client, she felt responsible somehow. And because Dad had put her in charge temporarily, that definitely made her responsible for what happened on her shift.

She couldn't fail her father. Not when he needed her to take over the spa one day. Not when he was grooming her for it.

She heard the click of a door. Soft. Unmistakable.

No one was supposed to be here. The guards didn't walk this area of the spa, just the research labs in back.

Another soft click.

She wasn't alone.

Her throat closed up and she couldn't breathe. A part of her screamed to do something, even while a smaller, rational part of her argued that it was probably a guard doing a more thorough check of the building than usual.

A shuffle. Several shuffles.

There was more than one person.

She jumped to her feet. Her shaking hand reached into her desk drawer even as she eyed her half-open door. The spa was completely dark except for her office. Whoever was out there would know she was here.

Her fingers curled around the solid, cool metal of the massive flashlight Dad had given to her for whenever the power went out. At the time, she'd laughed and asked him if it wasn't overkill, since the beam was brighter than the ones used by search-and-rescue units.

She wasn't laughing now. *Thank you, Dad.*

More footsteps. Still soft, as if trying to hide their presence.

She slipped from behind her desk and positioned herself against the wall, behind the door. She gripped the flashlight more tightly, and her nails scraped against the metal.

The door moved a fraction of an inch. They were right outside.

"Surprise!"

"Aieeeee!" she screamed

"Aaaaaaaah!" someone screeched.

Her flashlight dropped to the floor with a clatter.

Wide blue eyes peeked around the door at her. "Miss Grant? Are you okay?"

"Sarah, you scared ten years off my life!" She swallowed to get herself to calm down.

"We, uh…wanted to surprise you." Haley also poked her head around the door.

To give herself time, Naomi bent to pick up the flashlight. She laid it on top of the filing cabinet in the corner and gave the top drawer a sharp shove, even though it was already closed. Yes, she was, uh, filing. Not standing behind the door lying in wait with a flashlight the size of a club.

"We saw your car in the parking lot, so we knew you'd be here." Sarah entered the room, followed by Iona and Haley.

"We figured you were working all day."

"And we wanted to cheer you up."

"So we brought you dinner." Sarah held aloft a bulky paper bag with the familiar Luigi's logo on the side.

"That's so sweet of you. Thanks, girls." She took the bag from them, the scent of garlic curling up at her. "Were you out for your weekly dinner together?" It warmed her that the staff bonded with each other outside of work. It implied that the spa had created a family atmosphere where friendships formed, and not just a company of employees.

"No, we usually eat out on Monday nights."

"But we decided to go out again tonight since we were all off work."

"Do you know when the spa will open up again?" Iona asked.

Naomi shook her head. "Soon, hopefully." They couldn't lose too many days of packed appointments that had to be rescheduled or canceled.

"So, Miss Grant, did Dr. Knightley kill Ms. Ortiz?" Sarah's eyes were wide.

"What? Why do you say that?"

"We were at the receptionists' desk when he came in, but we heard him ask for her," Iona replied.

"And Ms. Ortiz never mentioned his name when she came to the spa before, and you know how she likes to talk to us staffers," Haley added.

Naomi fixed the threesome with a stern eye. "Have you been spreading rumors?"

"No, don't worry, Miss Grant," Iona said. "We were just talking amongst ourselves at dinner tonight."

"So, is he involved somehow?" Sarah asked.

"How does he know her?"

"Why did he ask to see her?"

"Dr. Knightley had things to discuss with Ms. Ortiz," Naomi said. The girls' habit of rapid-fire questions made her feel a bit harassed. How could she get out of this conversation?

"But what?"

"And why?"

"How does he know her?"

"Did he already know she was dead?"

"Do you think he killed her?"

"He didn't kill her—he's her ex-husband." Naomi regretted it the moment it came out of her mouth. Aunt Becca had said it wasn't common knowledge, but Naomi had been caught off guard by the girls' questions.

"Oooh." The three looked at each other in surprise and faint titilation, but not in maliciousness.

Their innocent expressions eased Naomi's guilt over letting that tidbit slip. "Please don't repeat that, girls."

"Oh, we won't."

"We promise, Miss Grant."

"We want the police to catch whoever did it."

"Oh, that reminds me." Haley snapped her fingers. "We came up with an idea."

"We were talking at dinner."

"Sarah came up with it."

"You know how Ms. Ortiz loves…er, loved to talk?" Sarah colored a bit.

Naomi nodded.

"Well, she always arrived early for her appointments so she could enjoy the Tamarind Lounge beforehand."

"And we had several Tamarind members who had appointments at the same time or before Ms. Ortiz's massage yesterday," Iona added.

"She might have said something to one of them," Haley chimed in.

"Said something?" They had a point. One of the women

she spoke to might remember something, even something that might seem trivial but provide a clue about why someone would want to kill her.

But what if it was just someone who wanted to discredit the spa? If so, and they were still out there… Naomi shivered.

"We can't exactly question the Tamarind members," Iona continued.

"But you can," Sarah said.

She could. Some women might have already left Sonoma, but she could pay a "goodwill" visit to some of them at their hotels, to assure them of the spa's continued gold-standard service despite the "unpleasantness" of yesterday, and she could probe them about what Jessica Ortiz might have let drop.

"Girls, do you know who—"

"We already did it for you." Iona smiled and handed her some printouts. "We went to the receptionists' desk when we let ourselves in."

"We looked up every Tamarind member who had an appointment before or at the same time as Ms. Ortiz."

"And we got their hotel information, too."

"You girls are worth your weight in diamonds." Naomi scanned the sheets. There were only five women listed.

The girls giggled. "I'd prefer just one huge diamond, like Sarah's." Iona sighed.

"How are your wedding plans coming along?"

They chatted a few minutes more, then her phone rang.

"Bye, Miss Grant. We'll leave you now," Sarah said. The girls waved as they left the office.

"Hello?"

"Miss Grant, it's Neal in security. There's a Detective Carter who wants to speak to you."

"He's here?"

"Standing outside the front doors."

"Let him in."

A trembling started in her stomach as she sat at her desk and waited. What next? Why would he need to see her again? If he were just looking at the crime scene again, he wouldn't have asked to see her.

A short knock on the half-open door, and his thinning red-gold head eased in. "Miss Grant?"

"Detective Carter. Come in."

He sat in the chair across from her and withdrew his notepad slowly. The action made her twist her hands in her lap. Why was she so nervous? She hadn't killed Jessica.

"Miss Grant, can you tell me your whereabouts at approximately ten-fifteen yesterday?"

"I had finished an appointment at ten. I think I was here, in my office."

"For how long?"

"A few minutes. Then Aunt Becca called me into the reception foyer for Sarah's announcement about her engagement."

"Do you know the exact time?"

"Not really. But we were there for about ten or fifteen minutes. Dr. Knightley came in around ten forty-five."

"Can anyone corroborate your whereabouts between ten and ten-thirty?" His eyes rose from his notebook and skewered her.

"You mean…I don't…I don't have anyone. I was here alone." From a little after ten until she went to the entrance foyer at around ten-thirty. She wiped her palms on her pants legs.

"No one called you?"

She shook her head. "Why are you asking me this now?

Why that time frame? Was that when…" Then it clicked. The coroner had established the time of the attack—ten-fifteen. That's why he was asking this now.

Jessica had been alive, but bleeding when they found her. When had that been? They probably had an exact time from the 911 call.

But it meant she'd been attacked earlier. Hadn't Ms. Cormorand told her that some nameless staff member had come for Jessica around ten-fifteen? And she had lain there bleeding until she was found. "Was that when she was attacked? Are you asking me if I attacked her?"

"I'm not accusing you of anything, Miss Grant."

This wasn't happening. *Oh, God, help me.* But where was God? He wasn't preventing this man from suspecting her of doing something so awful she couldn't even think about it without gagging. Last night, she hadn't slept well because she kept seeing Jessica's face and all that blood.

"I didn't kill her. Why would I kill her? And in my own massage room?" Her voice started rising, and she couldn't stop it. "I liked Jessica. I'm trying to do a good job taking over the spa while Dad's sick. This is going to devastate him. He's still too fragile. He—"

"Detective Carter, how nice to see you again." Aunt Becca's words were gracious, but her tone sliced through Naomi's panicked monologue. She was glad to see her but wondered why she'd come to the closed spa.

Naomi realized she'd risen to her feet, and she sat again. She bit her lip—maybe that would prevent more nonsense from spewing out. But it wouldn't do a thing about what she'd already babbled.

Aunt Becca smoothly inserted herself into the room and the conversation. "I hope the guards let you into the spa without trouble? We told them they could expect you at any time. May I offer you something to drink? A glass of water?"

"No, thank you, ma'am."

Aunt Becca laughed. "I thought you were calling me Becca." She gave Naomi a sidelong glance as if to ask, *Have you pulled yourself together by now?*

Naomi clenched her hands in her lap. "Detective Carter was asking me where I was between ten and ten-thirty."

Becca's eyebrows rose toward her coiffed bangs. "Is that when Jessica was…" She pressed her lips together. When she spoke again, gone were her dulcet tones of a moment before. "Detective Carter, my niece had an appointment that ended around 10:05 or 10:10. She was here in her office when I called her at around ten-thirty to come into the reception foyer. She wasn't breathless from racing from the women's locker room after changing out of a bloody spa uniform and scrubbing blood from herself."

He didn't say anything, but his eyes met hers in a long, steely gaze.

"And I," Aunt Becca continued, "spoke to more than a dozen people between ten and ten-thirty. I can give you their names if you like." Without waiting for an answer, she grabbed a pad of paper and a pen from Naomi's desk and started scribbling.

Detective Carter sat silent, motionless. Unfathomable.

Aunt Becca finished with a flourish, tore out the page and handed it to him. "Are you quite done, Detective?"

"Yes, ma'am." He rose and left.

Naomi let out the breath she'd been holding. "Aunt Becca, you shouldn't make him mad."

"The nerve of him. You don't have a motive for killing Jessica or ruining the spa's reputation."

"I guess he still has to ask."

"There are lots of people who didn't like Jessica Ortiz. And there are certainly several people who don't like your father, either, who'd be happy to see the spa go out of business."

"But were any of them inside the building yesterday?"

"I wish we had the outside surveillance tapes. We could see who had entered the spa yesterday morning."

"I wonder if they found the man who ran away last night."

"Exactly. Why wasn't he asking you more about him, rather than insinuating that you'd killed your own client?"

Good thing Martin had been there. And Devon, though she didn't want to admit it. "Do you think he's questioned Devon Knightley, too?"

"Undoubtedly." Becca stopped her pacing and dropped into the chair the detective had just vacated. "But he's as innocent as you are."

"Are you so sure of that? She was his ex-wife."

"And they had a very nasty divorce. She wiped him out, which was just spiteful considering how much money her family already has."

"She did? He's in financial trouble?"

"Not anymore. He's been slowly recovering from the financial devastation she caused him. He's a very good doctor, you know. At least, that's what his mother says."

"And of course she's unbiased."

"He wouldn't be the orthopedic surgeon of the Oakland Raiders if he weren't good."

That was true. "So he hated her. He had a strong motive to kill her. Why do you think he didn't do it?"

"I know him, I know his family—"

"You said that before. But he could have found a way

to sneak into the spa, attack Jessica, then sneak out, come around to the front and enter, demanding to see her."

"Think back to yesterday. Did he look like he'd dashed from the back of the spa to the front in this heat?"

No, he'd looked calm, masculine and heart-stopping.

"And why would he walk in and announce himself to be in the same building as a woman he'd just attacked?"

"To avert suspicion?"

"Besides, the bloody uniform was female and the clothes were in the women's locker room."

She hadn't thought of that. A part of her uncoiled in relief.

But why should she be relieved? Why should she care about him?

And considering how Jessica had cleaned him out in that messy divorce, he probably didn't want anything to do with women, much less solvent women. Because of her father's business savvy and investments, the Grants were even wealthier than the Ortizes.

"Come on." Aunt Becca jumped to her feet. "I came to the spa to take you out to dinner. We could use a break."

"But Iona, Sarah and Haley came by earlier and brought me dinner." She motioned to the still-warm bag on her desk.

"That's nice of them. But you don't want to eat alone right now—or, rather, I don't want to eat alone right now. Put it in the staff fridge and let's go."

"I wouldn't be very good company right now."

"Neither would I. Let's cheer each other up before we have to go home and face your father."

Devon exited the front doors of his hotel and headed next door, across the parking lot of Alexander's Steak

House. He was so hungry that his stomach pulled painfully toward his spine.

Headlights blinded him momentarily. A car zoomed past him, rather recklessly for such a small parking lot.

He'd never take his admin for granted again. Martha had surprised him this morning by showing up at his hotel door with his laptop and a stack of files. She'd worked with him all morning, leaving him with, "I'll be praying for you." This time, for some reason, the phrase didn't make him want to roll his eyes. Hopefully she had been okay driving the three hours back to her home in the South Bay.

Prompted by a sharp pain in his belly, he hurried as he wove through empty cars. As he emerged from between two cars, a bright light made him blink and squint. The car that had zoomed past him earlier now sat idling down the aisle of the parking lot, headlights blazing. Waiting for someone?

He walked along the edge of the aisle as he headed toward the restaurant entrance, keeping the way clear in case the car decided to drive toward him and out of the parking spot. But instead, it slowly stalked him, like someone following him in order to get his parking slot. Except there were plenty of empty stalls. His hackles rose. What was going on? He glanced back again, but the car continued to follow behind him, not too close, but obviously the driver was not going to pass him. He couldn't see the driver because of the headlights, but he thought the car was white.

He walked more slowly. The car slowed.

He walked faster. But the car's pace didn't change.

The car was several yards back. He stopped, indicating that he needed to cross. The car stopped.

He crossed.

The engine roared. Tires squealed. The sound rumbled through him, making his heart lurch. The headlights hit him right in the eyes, making his world turn white. His brain told his feet to sprint to safety, but somehow his body wasn't responding fast enough. His leg muscles bunched as if wading through water. *Move! Move!*

He flung himself forward. Wind from the passing car whipped at his ankles.

He crashed into a large terra-cotta pot containing some ornamental shrub, and leaves rained down on him as the pot wobbled. The ground was still warm with residual heat from the day, and the acrid smell of asphalt rose with the warmth. Sharp stones dug into his side where he lay. As he dragged in a few breaths, he noticed the throbbing in his shoulder and upper back. Probably where he connected with the pot.

From far away, he heard cries and shrieks. Then a strong hand at his shoulder. "You all right?"

He rolled over and sat up gingerly. More than just his shoulder hurt—it seemed as if every bone ached from the jarring. "I'm fine."

"Are you hurt?" A young Hispanic man crouched beside him, dressed in the uniform of a valet.

"I just ache a bit."

"Want me to call a doctor?"

"Devon!" A cloud of something fresh, exotic and soothing at the same time was the only warning before Naomi Grant was on her knees in front of him. "Are you all right?"

"I'm fine. What are you doing here?"

"We saw everything." Becca Itoh appeared beside him. "We were on the sidewalk, heading toward the restaurant."

"I was at the other restaurant across the street," the Hispanic man said. "The car was a white Lexus driven by a woman—I got a look as she turned onto the road."

"Carlos, thank goodness you were working tonight." Becca touched the man's shoulder briefly.

Devon eyed the gesture. "You know each other?"

"Our families have been friends since Carlos and Naomi went to kindergarten together," Becca replied.

"This isn't some random accident," Naomi said, dialing her cell phone. "Not with everything that's been happening. Detective Carter needs to know about this."

"I got a partial license plate number, too, Naomi," Carlos said.

Only then did it fully hit him. Someone had deliberately tried to run him down. Someone had tried to kill him. His sore muscles suddenly didn't seem so bad. It could have been so much worse. He could be dead.

Naomi clicked her phone shut. "The detective is on his way."

"The guy must think we have him on speed dial."

"Why would anyone want to hurt you?" Becca asked.

Why *would* anyone want to hurt him? he wondered. His assets were nothing like they used to be, thanks to Jessica, and he didn't have any disgruntled patients who were so mad they wanted to kill him.

"It seems odd." Naomi's voice was low, tentative.

"What do you mean?" He tried flexing his arms, his legs. Nothing serious. Maybe he could stand up.

"You. This. That car."

"Maybe it's not just Jessica—maybe someone's after people connected with her."

"An ex-husband?" Becca snorted. "Seems far-fetched."

"I'm starting to think it's not about Jessica," Naomi said.

"Why?" He didn't like the strained look on her face, a mix of stress and fear.

"I think it's about the spa. Or me."

Something fiercely protective rose in him. "Why would you think that?"

"If we hadn't been here tonight…"

"This would still have happened."

"But if we hadn't been here, then I'd have been the first person Detective Carter would have called."

"What do you mean?"

"I own a white Lexus."

SIX

Someone was setting her up.

She shivered for the hundredth time. Someone hated her so much, he or she was trying to frame her. Nothing direct, but things blatantly pointing to her.

Who would do this? She wasn't Miss Congeniality, but she didn't have any enemies she could think of who'd go to this extreme.

Naomi stood to the side as Detective Carter spoke to Carlos. She'd endured a stressful grilling by him—after all, here she was present at the scene of yet another crime.

She peered around the corner at the ambulance, which was blocking access to most of the parking lot. Devon still sat on its tailgate, where a paramedic checked his sore ribs.

At first, when she and Aunt Becca had been walking down the sidewalk and she'd seen Devon's dark figure in the parking lot, she'd fought down rising excitement—the first joyful feelings she'd had in two days. But only for the moment it took her to remember that he was hiding something—maybe something important.

She couldn't be sure if he was involved in Jessica's murder or not.

And now, waiting for a chance to talk to him, her heart wouldn't stop pounding. Because while it scared her to the core that someone wanted to hurt her, a part of her was profoundly relieved that that someone wasn't Devon.

Her attention strayed back to Carlos. Detective Carter had finished talking to him. In fact, Carlos was just ending a call on his cell phone. She wandered over to him.

"How are you doing, Carlos?"

He nodded and smiled. "Doing okay. Carmella's starting to show."

"That's great." She cast a furtive glance at Detective Carter, a few feet away with his back turned toward them, and lowered her voice. "Did you see the woman driving the car?"

"Just her profile, and I only got a glimpse when she passed under a streetlight."

"But it was definitely a woman?"

He nodded. "Do you think it has to do with Ms. Ortiz's death?"

She wasn't surprised Carlos knew about Jessica— Sonoma was a small town despite the tourists who flocked to it. She said, "It seems a little too coincidental, don't you think?"

"I think I recognized the car."

"You did? From where?"

"I've valeted the Paiges at the restaurant several times."

"The Paiges?"

"A dentist and his wife. I thought the license plate number was theirs."

"Are they at the restaurant now?" She glanced across the street at Evergreen, the Pinecrest Hotel's restaurant. The other valet was faithfully at his post, but craning his neck and trying to figure out what was going on.

"No, but I called Jerry, one of the valets at Papillon—the Paiges often go there to eat dinner when they're in Sonoma."

"Do you think they might be there tonight?"

He shrugged. "It's worth a shot, isn't it?" His cell phone rang. "It's Jerry. Hello?… Really? Aw, man… Yeah, I'll tell the detective. Thanks. Bye."

"Their car was stolen?"

"The keys were still on the valet's pegboard, but their car is missing from the lot. Whoever took the car must have broken in." He glanced over at the detective. "I didn't mention it to Detective Carter when he questioned me because I wanted to call Jerry first, but I should tell him now."

"Wait, before you go…you mentioned the couple's last name—Paige. Is the dentist's wife named Marissa Paige?"

"Yes. Do you know them?"

"She's a regular at the spa. In fact…" Naomi searched her memory. "I think she had an appointment that morning when Jessica…" She still couldn't say it, as if saying it made Jessica really gone.

Carlos was silent a moment, too. "I'll talk to you later, Naomi."

"Thanks a lot, Carlos."

Was there a connection between the Paiges and Jessica? Were they somehow involved in Jessica's death? Especially when Marissa Paige might have been in the spa the morning Jessica was killed?

Or maybe their car was taken because Naomi drove a white Lexus, too.

She shuddered. Was someone spinning a web around her, trapping her into a crime she didn't commit? Why would anyone want to do that?

There was too much she didn't know. Tomorrow she'd check the spa records to see if Marissa Paige had indeed been there that morning.

And if she hadn't… What did that mean?

SEVEN

Had her father blackmailed someone? Naomi couldn't think of any other reason why the police were letting them reopen the spa tomorrow.

Dad denied any shady dealings, so maybe Aunt Becca had finally charmed her way into Detective Carter's good graces.

Regardless, there was a ton of work to do today.

Naomi had called Sarah and Iona that morning to ask the receptionists to come in. She left the entry foyer to escape the noise of both of them on the phone, calling clients who'd had to cancel to ask if they wanted to be rescheduled, and calling clients already scheduled for tomorrow to verify appointments. She made a mental note to remind them to call spa staff as well to make sure everyone came in tomorrow, but knowing them, they'd have already done it by the time she talked to them again.

Naomi entered the ladies' locker room. Everywhere was evidence the police had been here—furniture askew, black dust she assumed was from the forensic fingerprint powder, some trash here and there. The cleaning staff usually came at night, but she'd call and ask them to come in today during the daytime. At least the metallic blood smell had dissipated.

Jessica's blood. How could she be so callous and cold about it only a few days later? It seemed wrong to think about doing business as usual when a woman had lost her life in a room down the hall, when her blood had soaked the staff uniform and towels that had lain here.

The outer door opened with a sudden whoosh, making her jump.

"Naomi?"

"In here, Aunt Becca."

"Martin was looking for you. You're not answering your cell."

Naomi patted her pockets. She'd forgotten her cell phone in her office again. "I was working with Sarah and Iona for a while, then I came in here. We'll need a new basket for linens. The police took the old basket as evidence."

"I'll buy a new linen basket this afternoon," Aunt Becca said.

"Good, because after I'm done here, I want to make a few visits in Sonoma."

"Oh?"

"Yesterday, Sarah and Iona looked up the Tamarind members who had been here the morning Jessica was…" She swallowed. "The morning I found Jessica. Some of them might still be in hotels in Sonoma, and I thought I'd pay them each a personal visit."

Aunt Becca smiled. "A personal apology from the Joy Luck Life Spa management, soothing ruffled feathers…"

"And chatting about Jessica, and what she might have said to them that morning."

Her aunt nodded. "That's a good plan. They might say something that means something significant to you, whereas it wouldn't have meant anything to the police."

"I hope so." She regarded Aunt Becca. "Speaking of police, I saw you talking to Detective Carter last night for a few minutes. What were you talking about?"

"Devon Knightley."

"Oh?"

"Well, it was obvious that Devon being run over takes him off the suspect list."

Naomi sighed. "You trust him too easily. I still say he's hiding something."

"And I think it's nothing important."

"He could have arranged to get himself nearly run over." But in her heart, she knew it hadn't been that. It had been too close—so close, she had fully expected to see his body colliding with the car's bumper, and she'd screamed like a maniac.

Aunt Becca tilted her head as she thought about it. "He could have. Except he chose a rather empty parking lot to do it. He couldn't have known we'd be walking on the sidewalk just as the car tried to hit him."

"That's true. If I were going to stage an accident, I'd have chosen a place with more witnesses."

"If not for us, Carlos would have been the only witness, and an iffy one at that, since he was across the street." Aunt Becca gave a triumphant toss of her gray curls. "I told you he couldn't have been involved in that nasty business."

Naomi hadn't wanted to believe Devon capable of murder, but she wasn't about to admit it to her gloating aunt. "You were saying about Martin?"

"He found me and asked where you were. It seems important."

They headed toward the back of the building, to the security room where the two day guards sat, monitoring the exterior cameras. "Martin?" Naomi poked her head around the door.

He turned in his seat at the sound of her voice, then immediately rose to his feet. "Miss Grant. I'm glad you're here. I have something to show you."

He rummaged in a cabinet opposite the security monitors. "I never got a chance to tell you that morning they found Ms. Ortiz, and then I didn't see you until that evening when you came in to take that late appointment." He pulled several videotapes out of the cabinet. "And then after that guy showed up that night, the detective was right there and I didn't want to say anything in front of him."

He turned and popped one of the tapes in a playback machine to the side of the monitors. A previously dark screen flickered, then showed the front entrance of the spa, at night, illuminated by the front floodlight.

Martin gestured to the screen. "We made copies of the surveillance videos before we gave the originals to the detective."

"What?" Naomi and Aunt Becca said at once.

Martin's chin gestured toward Jared. "After you called us about Ms. Ortiz, we knew the police would want the surveillance videos, so we immediately made copies of all the tapes from that morning. It didn't take long. Then we gave the originals to the detective."

"But this is nighttime." Naomi pointed to the video playing on the screen.

"After that guy showed up that night, I made copies of the videos again before giving the originals to the detective. I wanted to tell you, but he was right there."

That's why Martin had been so antsy right after the detective questioned him that night. "And you were off work yesterday."

"Plus I didn't know if you were at work or not. I didn't have your personal phone number." Martin lowered his voice. "I also didn't want to be overheard by anyone at my home. The videos were here, and I didn't want anyone else to know we'd made the copies."

Was it wrong to copy tapes before giving the originals to the police? She didn't think so, but the action itself might seem suspicious. "Thanks, Martin. I wasn't in a frame of mind to see the videos yesterday anyway."

Action on the screen pulled her attention back to it. Martin and Penelope left the building, the swath of exterior light glinting off some jeweled clips in her hair.

A few minutes later, the stranger appeared on screen.

Martin paused the video. The picture skewed a bit, but she could see the stranger's pasty face, the wide eyes that looked nervous and agitated even from this still shot. He somehow looked more vulnerable here than when he'd been inside talking to her.

"He hadn't even known about Jessica's death when he came in the spa," she murmured.

"Which suggests he wasn't involved in her attack," Aunt Becca said.

"He was pretty desperate when he raced out of there," Martin said.

Naomi studied the picture. "I think there's something suspicious about him, but I don't think he killed her."

"But he still might know something about Jessica or about her killer," Aunt Becca said.

"Martin, can you print out a copy of this shot?"

His brow wrinkled. He looked at Jared. "Do you think…?"

Jared nodded. "I think I can. Give me some time." He ejected the tape and inserted it into another machine on the other side of the desk, then fiddled with some cords and wires at the back of it.

Martin inserted another tape. "These are all from the morning Ms. Ortiz died."

Died. The finality of it saddened her. She had to get used to the fact that Jessica Ortiz was really gone.

They spent the next two hours watching all the tapes—fast-forwarding through the places where no one came on camera.

The spa staff entered early that morning from the back entrance. So did Rachel and her research associates, who came through the back but would split off once they were inside to head to the laboratory. That area was sealed off with a sophisticated electronic card system to protect Rachel's research, since the skin care products she developed were proprietary and exclusive to the spa.

"I checked the card key logs," Martin mentioned, "and only staff entered or exited the labs as far as I can tell."

Then came the stream of clients through the front door. Naomi and Aunt Becca made a list of patrons' names and the time they entered or exited. Anyone Naomi didn't recognize her aunt did, and vice versa.

"There's Jessica."

The platinum-blond curls were light gray in the tape, but Naomi couldn't mistake Jessica's bouncy walk, her confident stride. The morning sunlight sparkled off the wreath of diamonds around her neck.

"She really had been wearing a diamond necklace," Aunt Becca said.

"And it was definitely gone by the time I found her." Was that necklace at the root of all this? If so, once the murderer had the necklace, why try to harm Devon Knightley? Or maybe that accident was completely unrelated.

"Eloise Fischer." The woman walked into view with her head high and arrogant. Even from the video, Naomi could almost feel the cool glitter of her eyes. She noted the time— only a few minutes after Jessica. The two of them would have been together almost from the moment they checked in until Jessica had been called out of the Tamarind Lounge by the murderer, who had been dressed in a spa uniform.

She had talked to several staff that day, asking if any of them had called for Jessica. She wasn't surprised when none of them had. And she could eliminate the staff members who had been with clients at the time.

A few more clients entered the spa. "Is that…Marissa Paige?" Naomi pointed to the screen.

A short, quick-stepping woman darted into view like a sparrow. She even glanced over her shoulder and backed up a step in a random way like a skittish bird. But whatever was behind her must not have alarmed her because she continued into the spa.

"The Paiges' car was the one stolen last night?" Aunt Becca asked.

"The white Lexus."

Was there a connection? Marissa Paige had been here the morning Jessica was killed, and then it was her car that was "stolen" by a woman who tried to run down Devon Knightley. Was Marissa Paige somehow involved in Jessica's murder? Or was there another reason her car had been stolen for the hit-and-run?

Or maybe Devon Knightley's accident wasn't connected to Jessica at all.

But that just seemed like too much of a stretch. Devon was Jessica's ex-husband. Marissa had been here at the spa when Jessica was killed. Then it was her car used to try to kill Devon.

"I'll have to find out what treatment Marissa had scheduled," Naomi said.

"She's also probably still in Sonoma. The Paiges always take a couple weeks here, and Marissa Paige tends to schedule several different treatments while they're here."

"So I could go to see her today maybe?" Naomi glanced at her aunt Becca. "I don't know if I'll be able to phrase my questions well enough…"

She patted her hand. "I'm sure you'll be fine. I'd offer to go with you, but one of us needs to be here to prepare for the reopening tomorrow. And the client visits we talked about really should be done today so that clients will be inclined to reschedule their canceled appointments for tomorrow or the next day."

Meaning, Naomi wasn't just to probe for information. As the daughter of the owner of the spa, and acting manager, she was the face of Joy Luck Life, and first and foremost came her job—catering to their clients, apologizing for the inconvenience, encouraging them to continue their patronage.

They continued to watch the security videotapes. Very few women exited the spa. Most of the morning's clients remained for further treatments or simply relaxed and enjoyed the spa's lounges after their massage, facial or pedicure.

Then Devon Knightley walked into view. A strong, sure step. His head angled high, showing off the dark column of his throat. Naomi swallowed as she watched him cross the screen and enter the spa.

No one left after Jessica was found.

The tape ended. Martin reached for another tape shot from a different camera.

"Martin, did anyone else exit after that?"

"No. At this point, after we found out about Ms. Ortiz,

we had stopped the tape so we could make copies, and we put in a fresh tape for the video surveillance. We were watching the live feed carefully. Police came, but no one else arrived, and no one else exited until the detectives cleared everyone to go a couple hours later."

They watched the videos of the parking lots—both the staff lot and the valet lot—and the view from the valet station, which was a wide-angle camera that also caught some of the area to the side of the building.

No one snuck into the spa through the back entrance after the early morning staff had come in to work. No clients entered the spa from any entrance other than the front. No one broke into a side window or did anything else unorthodox.

After finishing the last video, Naomi sat back in her seat and rubbed her eyes. A knot had been forming in her stomach since she saw the video of the back entrance. The knot tangled and tightened as she watched the other videos.

This was not good.

Aunt Becca voiced her thoughts. "No one entered the building except staff and clients."

"Which means the murderer is one of them."

EIGHT

Someone had tried to get into her car.

Naomi glanced around the empty parking lot of the Valencia Hotel, then back to the mangled metal of her passenger-side door lock. How long had it been like that? She hardly ever opened this door from the outside. If she hadn't happened to get out of the car and forgotten to grab her purse from the seat beside her, she would have never gone around to open her passenger-side door from the outside—and discovered the torn-up lock.

She glanced around the hotel parking lot. There wasn't anyone around. Her heart picked up.

She was being silly. No one had threatened her life.

Yet.

She went back to the driver's-side door to get in and grab her purse. Her breathing quickened as she hurried out of the empty lot into the cool, air-conditioned foyer of the Valencia Hotel.

She stood near the entrance, trying to get her breath back. The handful of guests and staff milling around calmed her.

She was probably worrying about something that might have happened weeks ago. After all, she never turned on her car alarm when she parked at the spa because once, the alarm had gone off and guests had complained about the noise. She also trusted the valets to watch over the other cars in the parking lot as well as the clients' cars.

Except…no. It couldn't have happened weeks ago. She and Aunt Becca had carpooled to the evening service at church last Sunday. Aunt Becca hadn't mentioned the broken lock when she got into the car, and that was something her aunt would definitely have mentioned.

She'd have to ask Aunt Becca the next time she saw her. She considered calling her, but her nerves were too raw to talk about it right now.

She focused on her task ahead—to talk to Marissa Paige.

Who might or might not have killed Jessica Ortiz.

What was she thinking? Visiting a client alone when they knew the murderer was either a client or one of the spa staff? But who could she call?

She dialed Aunt Becca anyway.

"What is it, dear? I'm a little busy."

Naomi bit her lip. "Um…"

"What's wrong?" Gone was her aunt's brisk tone, replaced by a softer voice.

"I think…my car was broken into."

A sharp intake of breath. "Are you sure?"

"Did you notice the lock on my passenger side was broken when you got in my car Sunday night?"

"No, definitely not."

"So it happened sometime between Sunday and today."

Naomi tried to allay her rising panic by watching the guests in the hotel lobby—the elegantly coiffed woman sitting in a leather couch, the businessman at the counter, the pair of casually dressed tourists poring over a brochure of wine country.

"Where—no, over there, Sarah, and make sure it's stable." Naomi heard a gentle thud in the background. "Naomi, sorry about that. Where are you?"

"I'm at the Valencia Hotel."

"I could have believed that your spa room and the white Lexus were coincidences, but this has gone beyond coincidence. You shouldn't talk to Marissa Paige alone."

Good, at least she wasn't the only one being cautious. She refused to admit she was bordering on paranoid. "But you're busy."

As if to prove it, Aunt Becca fired off a few more requests to Iona and Sarah. "Iona, can you pull up these files for me? Thanks. Naomi?"

"I'm here."

"Call Devon Knightley."

"What? Are you out of your mind?"

"What do you mean? We know that whoever attacked Jessica was either a staff member or a client. He's neither, plus he never entered the spa before we saw him."

"We don't know that the murderer worked alone in this."

"Someone tried to kill him. Isn't that enough for you?"

"We still don't know for sure if that was staged or not."

Aunt Becca huffed. "You are paranoid. And you need to 'fess up. Why are you so skittish around Devon Knightley?"

"I'm not skittish." *I just think he's the most attractive man I know. And he's hiding something. Bad combination.*

"He's never been rude to you or anything like that?"

"No. But why do you trust him so implicitly?"

Aunt Becca sighed. "I don't really know. It's just a feeling I have. And when I prayed this morning, I felt God nudging me to pray for him."

"Pray for what?"

"He's searching, Naomi. Even if he doesn't know it. And wouldn't it be good for him to have a Christian showing him the love of Christ?"

Everything had been so crazy lately—and even before then, with Dad training her to take over the spa. She wished she could be a massage therapist again, not acting manager and the one responsible in the face of all these troublesome events. But she wasn't about to disappoint her father, and she was very glad she had Aunt Becca to help her.

Aunt Becca was still directing the staff around her. "Thanks for coming in, Haley. There's plenty to do. You can start by helping Iona with the reservations."

"Why don't I call Rachel and ask her to come with me instead?"

"You know your sister won't leave her experiments. And don't even think about Monica, because she's taking care of your father."

And Aunt Becca was taking care of things at the spa. "Fine. I'll call him."

"Just think of it this way. Who do you trust more— Marissa Paige or Devon Knightley?"

With her life?

Devon.

But she didn't trust him with her heart.

Naomi knocked on the hotel room door of a possible murderer, while Devon stood at her side.

He'd been a little surprised but gratified that she'd called him to accompany her—after all, this was the woman whose car almost hit him.

The door opened.

"Mrs. Paige? It's Naomi Grant."

"Come in, come in," the woman said, swinging open the door.

"This is…" Naomi stared at Devon a second. "Devon Knightley, a friend of my family."

The corner of his mouth quirked.

"So pleased to meet you." Marissa's hand drew his attention from Naomi and erased the quirk.

Marissa beckoned them to the apricot-and-cherry striped couch in the suite's living area. "I was so surprised when you called and wanted to see me."

"I just wanted to extend Joy Luck Life Spa's personal apology for the events that happened a few days ago."

"Oh, I couldn't hold the spa responsible for something someone else did." Marissa sat in an overstuffed armchair in a peach floral design that was adjacent to the couch. "Can I get you anything?"

"Nothing, thanks." Naomi stared at her folded hands. "Um…the spa is reopening tomorrow."

"Oh, how wonderful." Marissa's eyes glittered, tiny and black.

"I'd like to personally offer to reschedule your canceled facial."

Marissa flitted to the sideboard so fast, Naomi blinked and she was suddenly across the room. She rummaged in her purse, pulling out half its contents until she found her appointment book. Typical of her—at the spa, she always spread her things all over the receptionists' counter when trying to find her wallet. Marissa darted back to her chair with her appointment book.

"Donald and I are going wine tasting tomorrow. We have an appointment to do a food and wine pairing at Kendall-Jackson. But maybe the day after?"

"Three o'clock?" Marissa usually scheduled her appointments for midafternoon, and Naomi had called Sarah to keep facial appointments free from two o'clock to four o'clock specifically for Marissa.

"That would be perfect." Marissa wrote the time down in her appointment book.

"As I understand it, you were in the Tamarind Lounge with Jessica Ortiz that morning. How…um…shocking for you." She hoped she instilled the right amount of concern in her voice.

Next to her, Devon cleared his throat.

Marissa's eyes flashed up at her, wide and startled. "Oh, it was so horrible to hear what happened!"

"Did you speak to Jessica while you were with her?"

"A little…" Marissa bit the inside of her lip. "We weren't…friends, exactly."

"Did she seem to be acting strangely at all?"

Marissa blinked rapidly. "How funny. That's what the detective asked me that morning."

Naomi hadn't meant to sound like an interrogator.

Devon slid into the conversation. "Just think, you could have been one of the last people to speak to her." His voice resonated with empathy.

Now it was Naomi's turn to clear her throat.

Marissa's shoulders rose and fell in a deep sigh. "How awful. How tragic."

"Did she say anything to you?" Devon's expression radiated compassion.

"Not really. She was so full of joy—you know how she is." Marissa flashed a smile at Naomi. "She kept fingering that diamond necklace—"

"Necklace?" Devon's voice cut through the reminiscent atmosphere. "What kind of necklace?" His eyes had started to burn with intensity.

What was the significance of Jessica's necklace to him? Naomi wondered.

She realized that he hadn't even been aware that Jessica had been wearing a necklace until now. He also didn't know that Jessica's necklace had been stolen. After all, the detective had learned about it after he spoke to Devon, and it wasn't something he would have even mentioned to the victim's ex-husband unless he were going to accuse Devon of something.

Was it something she ought to tell him about?

But he was keeping secrets, too. She'd keep this bit of information to herself, just in case.

"She had a beautiful necklace," Marissa was saying. "But I don't really remember it well. She always had on some type of lovely jewelry. I think it was diamonds and pearls."

Naomi almost corrected her that it was a Tiffany diamond necklace, but stopped herself just in time.

Devon seemed to deflate. While he still looked at Marissa, his gaze was unfocused. "It's true, she loved jewelry. She always had on something beautiful and expensive." His tone was low, neutral, almost as if he were speaking to himself.

Marissa jumped to her feet. "I'm sorry to rush you off, but I'm supposed to meet my husband…"

"Oh, I'm sorry for keeping you," Naomi said, standing. "Thank you for agreeing to see me for a few minutes." As she followed Marissa to the door, she remembered to say, "Mrs. Paige, I heard about your car. Did you ever recover it?"

She held her breath. It was a gamble, but hopefully Marissa wouldn't have heard about who the car almost ran down—just that it had been stolen. And hopefully she wouldn't ask how Naomi knew about it.

"Oh! It was so awful!" Marissa shrieked. "The restaurant manager came to our table to tell us that our car had been stolen. And the keys were still in valet, isn't that strange?"

Marissa's face then glowed a rosy hue. "We did find the car, abandoned a few blocks away. And *my* keys were inside."

"Your keys? No one broke into it?" Now that Naomi thought about it, if someone had broken a window, the car's alarm would have sounded and alerted the valet.

"I don't know how, but someone stole my keys from my purse. I was all over Sonoma, so it could have been taken anytime. And then they followed us to take the car while we were in the restaurant." She sighed. "I suppose it was just a few kids out for a joyride. Nothing was taken, and there wasn't even a ding on it." Marissa squeezed Naomi's arm. "You're so kind to ask about it."

"When I found out, I knew you'd be concerned and…I'm glad it turned out to be nothing serious."

They said their goodbyes and by mutual consent paused a moment out in the hallway after she'd closed the door.

"Mrs. Paige had her keys the day before because she drove to the spa," Naomi said.

"I'm thinking the keys were stolen while they were at the restaurant," Devon replied.

"Anyone could have taken them—someone could have passed behind her chair and slipped a hand in her purse," she said, starting off down the hallway toward the elevator.

Devon kept pace with her. "There's a possibility she gave her key to whoever tried to run me down."

"But what would be her motive? She didn't even know you when you walked in. You didn't recognize her, did you?"

"No."

"Do you have any connection to her husband?"

"I'll have to call my admin to check, but I don't think so. I know I've never done surgery on him."

"No connection with the Raiders?"

"I do surgery on the players—I don't have a connection to anything else. And all my surgeries on the players have been successful. Nothing for anyone to complain about."

She punched the button for the elevator. "None of this makes sense. Maybe this isn't connected to Jessica's death at all."

He stood close to her, a little closer than he should, actually. His sandalwood cologne wove around her. Musky, spicy, exotic. It made her think of his strength, warriorlike. Strong enough to protect her.

She couldn't help herself—she glanced up at him.

He was looking at her. His eyes were dark and glittering. Glinting, almost hypnotic. He swayed closer. She could feel the heat of his body, contrasted with the crisp air-conditioning. He warmed her. He was going to kiss her.

And then he blinked. His eyes dulled and he backed away.

As they shared the elevator down to the lobby, she realized that she'd been mistaken. He hadn't been about to kiss her. She'd been delusional because she found him so attractive. She'd been guilty of the same thing she did every year at the Zoe dinner—reading more into his friendliness than was actually there.

Besides, she had a spa to run. She didn't have time for a social life. Plus, her life was here in Sonoma. He had a lively practice nearly two hours away in South San Francisco.

As a respected massage therapist, she'd toyed with the

idea of opening her own business, of moving away from Sonoma. But that was before Dad's stroke. That was before he needed her so much. Her family needed her.

So why did her responsibilities feel like a straitjacket?

He'd almost kissed her. Almost fallen down that path he'd vowed he wouldn't go. At least, not now. Not while his business was in such bad shape, not while Jessica's betrayal still stung.

But Naomi Grant isn't Jessica.

No, that deeper part of him was still too raw.

He had to stop leading Naomi on. He had to more clearly indicate that he wasn't interested in her.

Except that he was.

He had to stop trying to stand closer to her so he could smell that fresh, exotic, soothing scent of hers. He had to stop leaning in to catch the subtle nuances of her voice.

He had to stop looking in her eyes…except they drew him, stronger than the magnetic field of an MRI machine.

They reached the parking lot. "Do you want to take your car or mine?"

Surprisingly, she paled under the hot July sun. "Why don't you drive?"

"What's wrong?" He stepped close enough to see the pulse beating at her throat—faster than normal.

She glanced at the parking lot while her hands pulled at the edges of her blouse. "It's my car. Someone broke into it."

"What? When?"

"I don't know when. Sometime between Sunday night and now."

"You mentioned that you have a white Lexus."

She nodded.

"The same as Marissa Paige."

She nodded again, but slower.

"So someone could have tried to steal your car in order to run me down. But failing that, they took Marissa's car instead. Both white Lexuses."

He took her by the shoulders and turned her to face him. "Someone could be trying to set you up. Jessica's murder in your massage room. Your car—or, at least, one similar to your car—used to run me down, maybe another murder."

Suddenly the threat to his own life seemed paltry compared to the insidious web being woven around Naomi. He had to find a way to keep her safe.

She blinked, looking into his face, then shrugged his hands away from her shoulders. "What can you do about it?"

What could he do about it? What right did he have to do anything about it?

Her chin lifted as she stood there, challenging him with her silence. Finally, she turned and walked toward the parking lot. "Let's go. I still have clients to visit this afternoon. I told Ms. Alaveros I'd be at her hotel by four."

He followed her as she marched on, back straight, firm and determined, despite how frail she seemed.

He shouldn't get involved.

But he was already involved.

At least, that's what his heart was telling him.

NINE

The next day, nervousness suffused the air at the spa, stronger than the aromatherapy essences. It impacted everyone—staff and clients.

While Naomi's clients relaxed once they were in her new massage room, in the hallways they walked a little faster than normal, their eyes darted around them, and they didn't chatter as much in the lounges. At least, Naomi didn't hear as much chatter as usual when she walked into the lounges to collect her next appointment.

Her feet ached a little from walking through downtown Sonoma yesterday with Devon. She'd visited two other Tamarind clients who had been in the lounge with Jessica, but neither of them remembered anything more than what Marissa Paige had told her. While she'd improved the spa-client relationship with those women, she couldn't help feeling that all those hours had been wasted.

Well, not entirely wasted. She'd spent more time in Devon Knightley's company than ever before.

When speaking to the other clients, he'd been as charming as when they'd talked to Marissa. The women flirted with him and were more open to his questions. Naomi had to admit that he'd been very helpful.

And in between visiting those women at their hotels, he'd been an entertaining companion. His stories were funny but not malicious; most often they poked fun at himself rather than others.

Once in a while, a stronger look in his eye stopped her heart. It would last for a moment, a few seconds…and then it would disappear, and he'd be the friendly but slightly aloof Dr. Knightley once again.

Those hot-cold mixed signals were starting to irritate her. But she had to push Devon out of her thoughts because she had more important things to worry about. Like the spa's reopening after such a scandalous event.

At one o'clock, she had just escorted her completed massage client back to the main lounge when she saw Eloise Fischer about to enter the Tamarind Lounge. Her heart kicked into high gear as she hurried toward her. "Ms. Fischer."

She paused, her hand on the knob of the open lounge door. "Yes?"

Naomi met the eye of another massage therapist heading toward the lounge to collect her next appointment. Naomi had a one o'clock client, as well, but she could wait. Talking to Eloise Fischer about Jessica was more important. "Won't you come with me into the Anise Lounge?" She gestured toward a corridor lined with elaborately scrolled doors, each of them a private lounge for the spa's most elite members, Saffron clients. Luckily, she had remembered the Anise Lounge was available, since only a handful of clients could afford the Saffron membership, which included use of the private lounges. She knew that none of the Saffron clients were here today.

Ms. Fischer must have known about the Anise Lounge because her eyebrows disappeared into her coiffed gold-streaked bangs. She blinked, then broke into a gracious smile. "Why, thank you, Miss Grant." The condescension oozed from her voice as if it were she conferring the unexpected favor, rather than Naomi.

Naomi kept her polite, plastic smile fixed on her face. She'd dealt with people like Ms. Fischer too often for it to bother her anymore. Plus, putting an uppity client in her place wasn't in the job description.

Before leading Ms. Fischer down the corridor, she nodded to the other massage therapist, who still stood outside the Tamarind Lounge, her eyes wide at the unusual exchange. "Annalisa, will you tell Ms. Vogts that I'll be a few minutes late for her massage? And in case I don't get to it, please let Iona and Sarah know that I'm running late and I'll be in the Anise Lounge with Ms. Fischer for a few minutes."

"Yes, Miss Grant."

She felt a little silly, but she wanted to let Ms. Fischer know that everyone else knew Naomi would be alone with her, and in which room. If, by any chance, Ms. Fischer was the murderer, this might deter her from more violence.

Naomi led the way down a corridor and opened the gilded door to a room swathed in azure blue silks that swayed lightly in the faint breeze from the air-conditioning. She led the way to the pair of navy blue chairs in the corner and pressed the call button on the wall next to one.

Iona's voice chimed into the room in soft, polite tones. "May I help you?" An excellent, neutral response since the receptionists knew no one was scheduled to be in this lounge today.

"Iona, this is Naomi Grant." She turned to Eloise. "May we get you anything? A glass of wine? We have an excellent bottle of Kendall-Jackson Stature."

Ms. Fischer nodded. "I'd love that."

"Iona, two glasses of the Stature."

"Right away, Miss Grant."

Naomi sat in the other chair across from Eloise. "Ms. Fischer, I just wanted to personally apologize for the unfortunate events that occurred the last time you were here." She must be getting better at this, because that didn't sound half as awkward as when she had visited Marissa Paige and the other clients yesterday.

Eloise affected a bored look, although Naomi could see the gleam of pleasure in her eyes. "How nice of you," she drawled, as if being escorted to one of the expensive private lounges happened to her all the time.

"I hope you weren't too upset by the ordeal?"

Her hand reached up to the neck of her robe. "It was very shocking."

"Yes, especially if you were good friends with Ms. Ortiz."

Her eyelashes twitched. "We were quite good friends."

Naomi kept her body from starting in surprise, although she felt a muscle tic in her jaw. They hadn't seemed like good friends at all. "I'm so sorry, then, for how upsetting this must be for you."

"Yes. So upsetting." Dramatically, Eloise sank back in her chair.

"How did you know Ms. Ortiz?"

"From various charity events. Actually, I know her mother better than I knew her. I frequent the Ortizes' boutique in San Francisco." An exclusive clothing line catering to high profile clientele, a bit like how Joy Luck Life Spa had risen in reputation and popularity with wealthy patrons.

"I don't know if you remember, but that morning, when I was looking for Ms. Ortiz, I spoke to you and you mentioned that you had chatted with her. Had she been acting oddly in any way?"

Eloise's mouth tightened. "Well, she was in high spirits, I thought."

"Oh?"

"It's strange, but in the times I've seen her here at the spa, she never talks about the men in her life. But this last time, she couldn't stop talking about her new boyfriend. She seemed so...happy."

New boyfriend? Was that the stranger who had appeared at the spa the evening she was killed? But why had he seemed so nervous when he was asking for Jessica? And why had he run? "Did she mention his name?"

"No, just that they were going wine tasting the next day, and she had arranged some private tastings at a few exclusive wineries."

Still no name to the stranger's face. Eloise's attention seemed to be wandering, so Naomi brought up the other topic of conversation she needed to know. "Someone else mentioned... I seem to recall something about her necklace..."

"Oh, that pretentious thing." Eloise batted her hand at the air. "As if a Tiffany necklace weren't commonplace these days."

Eloise Fischer had never worn one to the spa, but Naomi kept that thought firmly locked in her head. "She was proud of her necklace?"

"Went on and on about how expensive it was and that it had been a wedding gift."

A wedding gift? From Devon? Suddenly Naomi wasn't so sure she wanted to find it again.

"Thank goodness Gloria Reynolds got into that argument with her, or she would have gone on forever about it."

Naomi's heart blipped. Argument? With Ms. Reynolds? "What did they argue about?" Naomi must have seemed too eager, because Eloise's eyes narrowed as they regarded her. Naomi hastily added, "I had heard they were so close." If *close* meant they shared the same lounge with each other once in a while.

"Close? The two of them? Gracious, no. I respect that Gloria is a *businesswoman*—" her tone implied the opposite "—but doing business in a spa is simply rude."

"They were discussing business?"

"They were in the far corner of the Tamarind Lounge so I couldn't hear them—thank goodness—but I think they were discussing something about *money owed*." Eloise's mouth pinched at the affront, although Naomi wasn't entirely certain that Eloise was offended at their having been talking about money, or simply that they had been too far away for her to overhear them.

Money? And the necklace had been stolen. Was Gloria Reynolds more entrenched in this than she seemed? What had Jessica done to upset Gloria?

A tap at the door preceded Iona with a tray bearing two full glasses of a rich red wine.

Eloise sighed even as she eyed the wineglasses. "Such a shame. Jessica was as beautiful as her mother is. And no mother should have to bury her own daughter."

What an awful thought. Naomi shuddered. "Oh, look at the time." She rose to her feet. "I have an appointment. Feel free to enjoy the rest of the day in this room, Ms. Fischer. Your aesthetician will call for you here."

She left when Iona did, with Ms. Fischer smiling broadly at both the use of the luxurious room and the two glasses of wine.

"Iona, would you mind telling Ms. Fischer's aesthetician that she's in this room rather than the Tamarind Lounge?"

Iona dimpled. "No problem, Miss Grant."

"Thanks."

Naomi went to collect her one o'clock appointment— late—but her mind swirled. Jessica had been here in Sonoma with a man? Maybe his name had been on the hotel reservation together with Jessica's. The spa often asked for a guest's hotel so they could leave a message, if necessary. She could find out later today where Jessica had been staying, and she might also learn the name of who- ever had been staying with her

The argument with Gloria Reynolds was very interest- ing. When she had a spare moment, she'd see if Gloria had another appointment today or this week. Gloria tended to make several appointments with the spa every time she came into Sonoma, so there was a good chance she'd be in sometime soon and Naomi could then ask her about Jessica.

A part of her screamed to leave it alone, to let the police handle it. But another part of her needed to do something to try to escape this tightening net. Everything was pointing to her as Jessica's murderer. She couldn't stand here and let things fall into place around her this way.

She had to prove her innocence.

Later that evening, Naomi collapsed, exhausted, in her office chair. What a busy day.

She was almost glad that Virginia Cormorand had had nothing more to add to what Eloise Fischer had told her about Jessica. Taking clients all day as well as worrying about what Eloise had said tapped her energy completely.

She'd called Jessica's hotel to ask if there had been any

other name on the room reservation, but she had no luck there—only Jessica's name.

"Naomi?" Rachel's airy voice floated into the office through her open door.

"Ready to go home?" She was so tired that she was glad they'd carpooled to the spa early this morning.

Rachel drifted into the office. "I'm waiting on one more incubation period. Give me five minutes." But the way she slumped into the chair on the other side of Naomi's desk, it didn't seem as if she were in a rush to get back to her lab to finish up. She noticed the picture on Naomi's desk. "What's that?"

"I almost forgot about it. It was on my desk this morning. Andrew printed a picture of the stranger from the surveillance video."

"The guy who came by the night Jessica was killed?" Rachel studied the photo. "He looks nervous."

"He was nervous."

"I wonder what he's hiding."

"I've cleared my morning schedule for the day after tomorrow so I can go around downtown and show that stranger's picture to some shop owners and waiters."

Rachel checked the timer clipped to her lab coat pocket. "Do you expect to find anything?"

Naomi told her about how the stranger might be Jessica's boyfriend, the necklace and Gloria Reynolds's argument with Jessica. "I checked the schedule, and Gloria doesn't have a reservation until a few days from now."

"So you can talk to her then."

"I wish she were in tomorrow. I guess I'm just impatient."

"You are." She didn't say it maliciously, just stated it like the bald fact that it was. Typical Rachel. She started fiddling with a paperweight on Naomi's desk.

"Stop that, you'll mess up my papers…" Wait a minute. Those papers had been moved. She was sure of it. She'd stacked them neatly this morning, and now they were askew.

She looked around her desk and noticed that her pen container was knocked a few inches out of place and her stapler was facing the opposite direction.

She shot to her feet, her heart pounding.

Rachel gazed up at her with confused eyes. "What's wrong?"

"Someone has been touching things on my desk."

"Are you sure?"

She nodded, scanning the office. The plant on top of her filing cabinet had been moved, because its leaves now draped over the front of the drawer when, normally, she kept them draped over the side and out of the way.

"Maybe Aunt Becca…?" Rachel suggested.

"I could see her searching for something on my desk. But why move my plant? Why move my trash bin?" That, too, was a few inches out of place from where it always sat flush against the side of her desk.

"Did they take anything?"

Her purse. She dove toward her lower desk drawer, where she kept her purse when she was with clients. Oh, no. She'd forgotten to lock the drawer. Dad always harped on her about it, and she always forgot. She'd been so busy this morning, she'd dropped her purse in the drawer without thinking.

Her purse still lay in the drawer, although she couldn't be sure if it had been touched or not. She thumbed through her wallet. No cards missing, all her cash still intact.

Her heart slowed a bit. Maybe it had just been Aunt Becca going through her desk, looking for something.

"When was the last time you were in your office?"

"Only an hour ago. And I know things were okay then, because I opened the file cabinet to get a file, and the plant was the way it normally was, not like this."

"Then you were with a client?"

Naomi nodded.

"Call security," Rachel said.

"Huh?"

"See if anyone has left the building in the past hour. If anyone rifled through your stuff and left, they'd be on the exterior camera."

"Good idea," Naomi said, dialing.

"Miss Grant?" Martin answered. "What can I do for you?"

"Martin, who has left the spa in the past hour?" she asked, putting the call on speakerphone

"Let me double-check the tape…. An hour ago, Ms. Itoh left. And then no one else until a few minutes ago—your last client, I think her name is Ms. Mariczek."

"Yes, that's right. I escorted her to the outer door since all the other staff had left."

"About ninety minutes ago, Miss Grant's—er, Miss Rachel's lab assistant left."

Rachel nodded. "Stephanie."

"No one else in the past hour? Any other staff or clients?"

"I'm checking…no, Miss Grant."

"Thanks, Martin." She hung up. "Maybe I'm just being paranoid. It doesn't look like anything was taken."

"If nothing's missing, what *can* you do?" Rachel replied. "Maybe one of the receptionists was in here looking for something earlier."

But her plant hadn't been moved earlier when the receptionists were in the building. What could she prove? She swallowed. "It's probably nothing."

Rachel's timer went off and she stood. "Give me a minute to finish up, and then we can go. Aunt Becca said she had a surprise for dinner tonight."

A light tap on the door, then a message slipped under it. Devon looked up from his computer in time to see the folded notepaper slide to a halt on the carpet.

He went over to pick it up. It read:

Dear Devon,

I apologize for the late notice, but wondered if you'd like to join us for supper tonight at eight o'clock. I would have called you, but my cell phone battery is dead and I'm on my way home, so I'm going to give this note to the porter to slip under your door. I hope you get this note in time and can join us. No need to call ahead, just show up. Directions to the house are below.

Naomi Grant

This note seemed odd in light of everything that had happened lately. Perhaps the true person behind this was Becca Itoh or Naomi's father, Augustus Grant. It could be that Augustus wanted to speak to Devon, and a family dinner would provide the opportunity to do so privately.

Regardless, he'd see Naomi again—although he knew that the more time he spent with her, the harder it would be to break off whatever was starting to grow between them.

He couldn't get into another relationship. Jessica's betrayal still nagged at him. Sometimes he would think he was doing fine, but then the bitterness would rise up in him, and he'd feel like he'd been gutted all over again. He wasn't going to risk going through that again.

He was afraid.

He knew Naomi wasn't Jessica, but he'd still be risking his heart and still be vulnerable. He could never enter a relationship with someone like Naomi Grant with only a part of his emotions. With Naomi, it would be all or nothing— she'd expect that. She'd bring it out of him, that whole-hearted feeling and commitment. She was that kind of woman.

He was not the right man for her.

So he fingered the invitation, wanting to go but knowing he shouldn't.

Stay away from her.

He saw her bright smile.

You need to do the right thing, make the right decisions.

He saw her exotic hazel eyes, tipped at the edges from her Japanese mother, amber-gold in color from her Caucasian father.

Face it, she frightens you.

But not as much as she intrigued him.

He checked his watch. Seven-fifteen. He had just enough time to make it to dinner if he hurried.

In backing out of his parking spot, he noticed that the brakes were a bit soft. Strange. He'd gotten the car serviced just a couple months ago.

The Grants lived north of Sonoma, close to Geyserville. Here were more remote vineyards, as opposed to wineries—the vineyard owners often sold their crops to the wineries rather than making wine themselves.

The roads became more curvy as he traveled farther

from the highway. Naomi's instructions were good, listing landmarks as well as road signs, but he still drove slowly so he wouldn't miss the roads. It wouldn't be good to be lost out here, especially as the sun started setting.

The road started to become hilly as he entered the rolling foothills. And then, as he was descending a particularly winding path, he hit the brakes to slow down…except he didn't.

He pumped the brakes, but nothing happened.

His heart thumped hard in his chest, almost painfully.

He took a turn too quickly. The steep embankment that fell away from the narrow road came too close to his tires.

He gripped the steering wheel more tightly. He had to stay calm. He had to try to control the car.

Another turn. Dirt shot away from the tires as he skidded a bit off the road. The steering wheel fought against him, and he hauled harder to keep the car in the turn.

He made it.

But he didn't make the next one.

He didn't yank the steering wheel in the other direction fast enough to make that next turn. Tires hit dirt, flinging up a cloud of dust. And then he was airborne for a breath-stopping moment.

He crashed hard back onto earth. And then he was hurtling down, down.

The car jolted as it hit grapevines. He bounced up and down in his seat, his head knocking into the car's ceiling. The steering wheel twisted in his hands, out of control.

Then suddenly he slowed and stopped.

He gasped in a labored breath. His chest ached violently. Was he having a heart attack? No, the seat belt had cut hard and deep across his torso and shoulder.

He sat there, just breathing. Glad to be breathing at all.

His hands shook with adrenaline as he fumbled for his cell phone. It had fallen to the passenger-side floor. He couldn't reach it. Then he realized that he had to undo his seat belt first.

Releasing the seat belt seemed to make it easier for him to breathe. He called Becca Itoh.

"Hello, Dr. Knightley. What can I do for you?"

"I need…" He couldn't seem to get enough air in his lungs.

"Devon? Are you all right?" Becca's voice had gone from polite to alarmed.

"My brakes went out. I went off the road, down a hill, into a vineyard."

"Oh my goodness, are you all right?"

"I think so. I need a tow truck."

"I'll call one. Where are you?"

He gave the road he was on, and the closest cross road he could remember.

"I'll get a tow truck to you right away. And we'll drive over there to pick you up."

"Thanks, Becca."

"What are you doing out here, if you don't mind my asking?"

"What do you mean? I got Naomi's dinner invitation."

He heard Becca murmuring to someone, heard Naomi's soft voice in answer.

"Devon…we never invited you to dinner tonight."

TEN

A short while later at the Grant house, Monica Grant, Naomi's younger sister, affixed a bandage to a cut above Devon's eye. "You might have a black eye tomorrow."

"How lucky you were so near our house," Becca said. "That way Monica can fix you up."

"He's a doctor, Aunt Becca." Monica collected the trash from the bandages. "He could probably fix himself up."

"But it's always better to have someone else do it for you. And it doesn't hurt that she's a nurse."

Monica's eyes rolled a little, but her aunt didn't notice. She got up from beside Devon on the couch.

Augustus Grant leaned forward and looked Devon in the eye intently. "Strange, your brakes going out like that." The stroke made itself known by Augustus's slightly slower speech. He didn't slur his words, but he spoke them at a slower cadence than Devon remembered.

"They felt soft when I left the hotel, but they were still fine. After I left the highway, I was driving slowly and didn't use my brakes much. But when I entered the foothills…"

"Those winding roads get steep quickly," Naomi said, entering the room and placing a mug of steaming coffee in front of him.

"When I was waiting for the tow truck, I looked under the hood at the brake fluid. It was low."

"A leaking brake line?"

"Except the car didn't pull to one side. One leaking line would make it pull, wouldn't it?"

"So…" Augustus's brow furrowed. "Leaks in all the lines at once?"

That meant sabotage. Not some type of wear on the car. Devon flashed to that awful feeling of being airborne as he missed the turn and went over the edge of the road. No, he had to focus. He was all right.

"Is that the note?" Naomi pointed to the coffee table at the message supposedly from her.

He was glad he'd thought to bring it with him. "Want to see it?" He handed it to her.

A frown marred her forehead as she read the note and sank into a chair across from him. "That's not my handwriting," she said. She shook her head as she set it back down on the table. "I'm sorry, Devon. I didn't send it."

"Although whoever did gave wonderful directions to our house," Becca pointed out.

"So it's someone who knows us. Who probably has been here." Naomi frowned and twisted her hands in her lap.

Augustus also frowned. "It's not hard to get directions to the house from the Internet."

"But how would they get our home address?"

"Are you kidding me?" Monica said as she reentered the parlor. "You can find almost anything on the Internet these days. Plus Dad's been doing a little business here at the house—yes, Aunt Becca, I'm monitoring him—so we've had lots of things delivered here rather than at the spa."

"So it could be anyone."

"Do you think Jessica's murder is definitely connected to these attempts to hurt Devon?" Naomi asked.

He didn't think Naomi realized the softness of her tone as she said his name. The mere memory of her voice curled his insides.

"How can it not be?" Monica said. "These events all point back to the spa."

"They all implicate Naomi in some way," Becca said, voicing what Devon had been thinking.

"Devon, are you going to report this to Detective Carter?" Naomi asked.

"No," he reassured her. "Besides, there's no proof it was sabotage."

"The garage will tell us later," Augustus said.

"Besides," Rachel said as she entered the parlor. "I was with Naomi from about seven o'clock. She can't be implicated in delivering the note." She bore a tray with Japanese-style handleless mugs and a gigantic teapot. "Anyone?"

Devon stared at his coffee. "Did you brew this just for me?" he asked Naomi.

She shrugged, although color seeped up from her collar. "I know you don't like green tea."

Her embarrassment warmed him more than the coffee.

"Is it…safe at the spa?" he asked, sipping his coffee. "You don't know if it was one of the staff, or a client, or someone who snuck in the back door."

"No one snuck in," Becca said as she accepted a mug of tea from Rachel.

Naomi looked sharply at her.

Becca's mouth formed a tiny O before she pressed her lips together.

"How do you know no one snuck in?" Devon asked.

"Oh," Rachel replied, "they saw the exterior surveillance videos."

Naomi stared hard at Rachel, who returned with a mild gaze. "What?" Rachel asked. "It's not as if he shouldn't know."

"Know what?"

"Our security guards made copies of the surveillance videos before giving the originals to the police."

Naomi's mouth tightened at her sister's airy answer, but she sat back in her seat, obviously defeated.

"So the only people you saw in and out—"

"Were staff and clients," Becca finished for him.

"So you know I'm telling the truth. About not killing Jessica," Devon said.

"I never doubted you," Becca said, but Naomi spoke at the same time.

"You have to admit it looked suspicious, your coming in to ask for her." She shrugged. "I didn't really know until we saw the video."

Her distrust stung. But he couldn't fault her feelings. It had looked suspicious. "Is that why you asked me to come with you to talk to Marissa Paige? You finally trusted me?"

She regarded him with steady eyes. "I trusted you enough."

His heart had been feeling like a twenty-pound weight in his chest ever since he heard about Jessica's necklace from Marissa Paige. Now it gave an awkward lurch. Maybe he should mention the necklace…

But he'd just gained their trust. No one else knew about it except his sister. And there was no guarantee Jessica had been wearing his mother's necklace in the first place.

But Naomi's piercing gaze made him want to spill everything, including how she made his heartbeat race when he saw her.

No. It was safer to keep his mouth shut, or he'd talk about more than just the diamond necklace.

"Well, I'm just glad you're unharmed." Becca interrupted his thoughts and Naomi's searching eyes. "God was watching over you."

Becca's religious talk didn't make him uncomfortable. God *had* been watching over him. The accident could have been much, much worse, and he could have had more injuries than just his aches and the cut over his eye.

If this kept up, he'd be covered with bruises from head to toe. His ribs and shoulder still ached from his near accident in the restaurant parking lot.

"God was watching out for you both times," Naomi said softly.

"Both times?" Monica's question snapped his attention back to the conversation.

"When he was almost run over," Naomi said. She bit her lip, and her eyes clouded. "That was horrible."

"It was frightening to witness," Becca said.

Maybe God had been watching over him then, too. But it was hard for him to fully believe—old thought patterns didn't change overnight.

His doubt must have registered on his face, because Augustus said, "Not convinced? As I recall, your father's a staunch atheist."

"Dad...likes to talk about religion. Or rather, the lack of it."

"I once spent an entire fund-raiser evening arguing with him about the existence of God." Augustus's eyes slid to Devon. "Is his son the same way?"

He answered honestly, because with this family, with

this man, he owed it to them. "Not lately. Not after seeing how your family has been handling everything that's happened."

Becca beamed. Naomi's cheeks turned rosy, but her eyes were serious.

"Jesus is always there for you," Becca said, putting a hand on his arm. "And He said—"

"Not now, Becca," Augustus said, although not unkindly. "Poor boy's been shaken up enough tonight."

But somehow, even Becca's fervor didn't grate on him so much. Something about this family's faith covered them like a protective shield. In their simple hospitality, in the way they accepted him. They didn't argue with him as his father did.

"Well, it's late, but why don't we eat dinner?" Becca stood. "And Dr. Knightley—" she winked at him "—I promise, this is a real invitation to dinner."

Naomi was being paranoid, but she couldn't help herself. As she entered her office near the end of the day, she checked to see if anything had been moved.

Everything was as orderly as she'd deliberately left it this morning.

She sat behind her desk, but the sight of her belongings didn't relieve her. It was as if the fingerprints of the person who had rifled through her office covered everything like an invisible film that she couldn't wipe away. Her office wasn't her own anymore.

The message light flashed on her phone. She'd better check her voice mail while she had a spare minute. But before she could, there was a light knock on her door. Devon appeared in the doorway, holding a box. He filled the small space, pushing out the shadow of whoever had invaded her office yesterday, making her feel sheltered and shielded at the same time.

"What are you doing here? It isn't safe for you," she said.

He smiled.

Her stomach flipped. Then she wanted to grab her words back—she sounded too concerned for his welfare than she had a right to be.

"You're here," he said.

"I work here."

"Someone here might also be trying to frame you," he said.

"Someone here might be trying to kill you."

His smile faltered, then turned rueful. "You got me there."

She nodded at the box he held. "What's that?"

"The reason I'm here." He set it down on her desk. "I went home."

"All the way back to South San Francisco?"

"Atherton, actually. My office is in South San Francisco." He was bent over the box, but he looked up at her with laughter in his eye. "I do have to work, you know."

"Oh." She'd almost forgotten, after having him around so much the past few days.

"I had to sign some papers, so I wasn't intending to drive back to Sonoma. But then I remembered this box in my storage shed. I'd been intending to give it back to Jessica." He laid a dusty high school yearbook on her desk. "I thought this was interesting. Jessica's family wasn't always wealthy. She came from a small town in Central Valley…I think it was called Glory."

Naomi eagerly flipped through the pages, a few sticking together from water damage and age. "There she is."

Jessica's wide eyes and even wider smile practically dazzled her from the black-and-white page. "She didn't change much, did she?"

Devon grew still, and Naomi glanced up at him. His face had closed, and his mouth was a grim line.

"What's wrong?"

He stared down at the photo for a long moment. "Nothing."

He looked sad and angry at the same time. Naomi traced Jessica's blond curls with a finger. "Did she change... while she was married to you?" It was a guess, but something in her told her she was close to the mark.

He looked away.

She remained silent, leaving him to this thoughts, but she reached out and touched the back of his hand where it rested against her desk.

He glanced down at where her fingers touched his skin, but he didn't pull away.

She wanted to run her finger across the worry lines in his brow, down the lines framing his mouth. Maybe soothe away the bad memories. How tragic to love someone and then have that love die slowly. Or maybe he hadn't loved her when he married her. No, she couldn't believe that— Devon would love fiercely, wholeheartedly.

She wondered what it would feel like to be loved like that. She wondered what it would feel like for *him* to love her like that.

Her spine melted and the pulse in her neck flipped. His skin burned her fingertips.

She pulled her hand away.

Naomi turned another page in the yearbook. "Aunt Becca would love looking through this." Her voice was thin and reedy in her throat.

"She already has." His voice was calm, sure.

She sighed inwardly. Her heart had turned over while he'd only felt the reassurance she wanted to give him. Well, that was probably for the best. "Has she? When?"

"She was in the entrance foyer when I came in, and she and a few of the other staff were picking through the box and looking at the yearbook for a few minutes."

"They must have gotten a kick out of it."

He smiled, and her stomach did another somersault. She put her hand to her belly to keep it in place.

"They were comparing hairstyles with what they'd had in high school."

She laughed, but it was higher-pitched than normal.

"When I found this, I thought Detective Carter might want it. But I wanted to give you a chance to look through it before I give it to him, just in case…" He shrugged.

She might as well look through it. She had no true connection to Jessica, and she didn't know why anyone would want to frame her for her murder. Something in the box caught her eye, and she peered inside. A pair of cheap women's heels with a broken rhinestone strap. There was also a glittery clutch made of cheap sequins, a dented prom tiara from some nameless accessories store, drugstore lipstick. She fingered a pair of long evening gloves—cheap polyester, if she wasn't mistaken. "Why did she keep these things?"

"Jessica was a pack rat. This was the most interesting box out of all the ones in the storage shed. There were seven boxes of old *People* magazines and five boxes of old clothes."

A knock at the door interrupted them and Detective Carter stepped inside the office. "Dr. Knightley, the receptionists said you were here."

Devon gave her a quick glance, full of meaning, and she instantly knew what he was trying so silently to tell her. She casually closed the book and slipped it under a few papers on her desk as Devon turned to the detective, his broad back shielding her actions.

"Did you need to speak to me?"

"Out in the hallway?"

When they left, Naomi picked up her phone to check her messages. Just one, from a San Francisco number she didn't recognize.

"Hi Naomi, this is Rayna Knightley, Devon's sister. I hope you remember meeting me. Anyway, forgive me for calling you, but I've been trying to reach Devon all day today, and for some reason his cell phone goes straight to voice mail. I know he was going to your spa this week to see Jessica Ortiz, and so I thought it wouldn't hurt to call you, just in case. If you do see him, could you please give him a message for me? I've been talking with my fiancé today, and while we were hoping I'd wear Mom's Tiffany necklace for my wedding, I've decided it's just not worth the trouble. I know he's still hoping to somehow get it back from Jessica, since it does belong to Mom after all, but he's been trying to get it back for months and she's just not being cooperative. So I'm going to wear my fiancé's mother's pendant…"

The rest of Rayna's message faded into white noise. Devon's mother had a Tiffany necklace? The same Tiffany necklace Jessica had been wearing when she came to the spa? Didn't Rayna know Jessica was dead? Hadn't Devon told her?

Was this Devon's big secret? Why wouldn't he have simply told her he was trying to get his mother's necklace back from Jessica? Why all the evasiveness, talking about "things from the divorce"?

The more she thought about it, the angrier she got. She needed answers.

She saved the message and marched out of the office. The hallway was empty, but she heard some commotion from the direction of the entrance foyer. What was going on?

"You're getting it all wrong." Devon's voice. She'd never heard it so strained before.

"Why don't you come down to the station with me so you can explain it?" Detective Carter said.

"You have the surveillance videos. You know I didn't enter the spa that morning to attack Jessica," Devon said, voice rising.

"I'd rather not discuss this here, Dr. Knightley."

"This is ridiculous. I didn't even know she'd been wearing the necklace."

Naomi entered the entrance hall, looking for Devon. There he was, glaring at Detective Carter. The detective's eyes were cool but steely.

"Devon—" she started to say.

He broke eye contact with the detective. The look he gave Naomi was intense, pleading. It frightened her. Her previous anger at him melted away.

Abruptly, Devon whirled and marched out of the spa, followed by the detective and a couple of policemen in dark uniforms.

Escorted like a criminal.

What had Devon done that made Detective Carter take him in for questioning? Naomi had stayed late, doing more paperwork, hoping to somehow erase the image from her mind and drown out the questions crowding her head.

She tossed down her pen. She should go home. She'd

read the same job application twice now and couldn't have said what the person's credentials were to save her life.

Her cell phone rang as she headed out the back entrance. It was probably her father. "I'm on my way home—"

"Naomi."

It was Devon. "What do you want?" she croaked.

"We need to talk."

How dare he call her now to explain. He could have explained everything to her several times in the past few days and he hadn't. "Talk? Finally? Now that you've been arrested?"

"I wasn't arrested. I was just brought in to the police station."

She fumbled at the knob to the back door. "You've got some nerve. I know about the necklace." The cool night air swept through the doorway as she exited the building. She wove her way through the shrubbery to the staff parking lot. "Why didn't you just tell me about it?"

"I was ashamed."

"Ashamed? I'd have to see it to believe it."

"Well, you can see it right now."

His voice hadn't come from her phone.

It came from a few feet ahead of her.

He stood in the pathway, blocking the entrance to the parking lot. He clicked his phone shut as she halted.

Her hand flew to her chest, trying to calm the hurricane inside. "What are you doing here?"

"Talking to you." The exterior floodlights crossed his face, making his eyes gleam. His mouth was soft but firm. "Naomi, just give me a few minutes."

She glanced over her shoulder at the exterior cameras, clearly visible from where they covered the staff parking lot.

His mouth pulled grimly to one side. "I suppose I

deserve that. I called Martin and let him know I was here and that I wanted to talk to you. He's watching us closely."

While it reassured her, she also felt faintly guilty for her action.

He gestured to the side, to the entrance to the ornamental gardens surrounding the spa building. "Walk with me?"

They strolled along the paved walkway, the air thick with the scent of the rose trees. But even then, she caught faint whispers of his sandalwood cologne, and it mingled with the sweet flowers to make her think of warm beaches, warm water, warm embraces.

They reached a fork in the path, and he paused at the trickling fountain. He didn't look at her. He reached out to catch the water dripping from the naiad's stone urn. "I'm sorry I didn't say anything, but I didn't know Jessica had worn a necklace to the spa—much less my mother's necklace—until we talked to Marissa Paige."

"Marissa was mistaken about the type of necklace, but I didn't correct her," Naomi said, turning her head away from him. "I knew you were hiding something and I didn't trust you the way my aunt did."

He sighed. She turned to look at him and saw him studying the water running through his fingers. "You had every right not to trust me." He pulled his hand back and rubbed his wet fingers together. "The reason Detective Carter brought me in is because they recovered some acidic voice-mail messages I left for Jessica a few days before she died."

"Messages?"

"I'd been trying to talk to Jessica for weeks. She kept ignoring my calls. Rayna's wedding was getting closer, and I was aggravated that Jessica wouldn't return a necklace that wasn't hers. It was as if she wanted to punish

Rayna as well as me. My messages grew angrier the more she ignored me. I threatened to hurt her."

That's why he'd been brought in, Naomi realized.

She turned to lean against the rim of the fountain and gazed at the lighted bulk of the spa, its gothic molding throwing strange shadows against the stone walls. "That doesn't explain why you were so evasive with me."

"After Jessica died, I realized how those messages would look. I figured Jessica had already erased them—I left them weeks ago—but I didn't want anyone to know about them. I didn't want anyone to know why I'd followed her to Sonoma." He sighed again. "And once she was gone, a part of me felt it would be disrespectful to let people know she'd stolen my mother's necklace. What was the point in muddying her name?"

He suddenly grasped her upper arms and angled her to face him. "Maybe I just wasn't thinking clearly after watching her die. Maybe with everything else that happened to me, my head was somewhere else. I'm sorry."

He was too close to her. His hands weren't tight on her arms, but his fingers burned into her skin. His eyes burned, too—straight into her, drying her throat, fueling a heat that rose up her neck.

His hands slid upwards. Paused at the pulse in her neck. Fingered her jawbone. Cupped her face.

Then his head descended, and his lips were on hers.

Cool. She had expected him to be warm. Hot. Burning. But he was sweet—gentle, almost tentative. Asking forgiveness with his kiss as well as his words. It curled in her stomach, made her reach out to him, try to convey the feelings she had for him that she couldn't voice. Couldn't ever voice.

He rested his forehead against hers. "Naomi."

She breathed him in, sandalwood and musk. And roses.

"I don't know where this is going. And after my divorce…"

He didn't need to say it. She could sense his fear. "It's too soon." Too soon for him. Too soon for them both to figure out what was happening between them. Too soon after everything happening at the spa.

"It's not. But it's…" He searched for words, but never found them.

"Someone's trying to kill you. Someone's trying to frame me," she said.

The piercing ring of her cell phone pulled them apart. She fumbled in her purse and checked the caller ID. "It's Dad."

"We'll talk when this is over."

But her vision of the future was too murky for her to contemplate.

Kissing her had made him feel complete.

Devon stared at his nightstand, images of last night flashing in front of him. She had forgiven him when he hadn't deserved to be forgiven. She had been peace in the midst of all these terrible events, even with the shadowy threat against her.

Devon was being drawn into her, and into her family circle because they were so inseparably a part of her. They were a family unit like he'd never known. And he wanted to be with them, as one of them.

He'd never felt that way about Jessica or her family. He'd never felt for Jessica what he felt for Naomi. Just one kiss, and his entire world had tilted.

True, Jessica had hurt him, and he still worried that Naomi could hurt him, as well. But something about her made the fear start to lessen.

He stretched, about to get out of his hotel bed to start the day, when his cell phone rang. It was Naomi. He couldn't stop the smile on his face as he answered. "Good morning, beautiful."

"G-good morning." Her voice sounded both surprised and tentative.

"Are you all right?"

"I…I wasn't sure if I should call you."

"I'm glad you did."

"I have the morning free, and…I'm going to go through Sonoma with a picture of the stranger who appeared the night Jessica was killed. I thought you might want to come along."

An entire morning with her. Maybe he'd be able to steal another kiss or two. "I'd love to."

"I also need to return that box and Jessica's yearbook to you. I looked through it, but there wasn't anything that popped out at me. You should give it to Detective Carter."

"Are you at home?"

"I'm about to leave. I'll meet you at your hotel."

"I'll be waiting."

"Oh, I forgot to ask you. Did you ever talk to the hotel porters about the note?"

"I did, yesterday morning before I went back to San Francisco. No one was asked to deliver a note to me. I'm thinking that despite what the note said, whoever wrote it walked up and slipped it under the door personally." That way no one would be able to trace a delivery to a porter, and none of the hotel staff would pay attention to someone who entered and left the hotel within a few minutes.

"Did you also hear back about your car?"

He wasn't sure he ought to tell her. He felt a fierce desire to shield her from the truth, to keep her from worrying. But he was done with deception. "The brake lines were tampered with to cause a slow leak."

Silence. He could imagine her worrying her bottom lip. "That's not good."

"I didn't get hurt. That's what matters. Let's just forget about it for now and enjoy our day."

"We're not on vacation. I want to try to identify this man."

"We will." But could they really do so when the police hadn't yet found him?

ELEVEN

He did manage to steal a kiss.

He arrived at the spa early and parked in the staff parking lot. When she pulled in, he was there to open her car door for her. As soon as she stood up, he clasped her around her waist and tenderly kissed her.

Her voice was breathless as she said, "You shouldn't do that."

"Why not?" His lips traveled down the column of her throat. That scent again—fresh, exotic, comforting. "What's your perfume?"

"I'm not wearing any."

"What am I smelling?"

"Oh. My soap—lavender, citrus and a little eucalyptus."

Comforting and fresh at the same time. "So answer my question. Why shouldn't I kiss you?" He raised his head to look at her.

Her irises were large and dark, and pink tinted her cheeks. "Because…with everything being so alarming and serious…" She swallowed. "I shouldn't be so happy."

He laughed, and held her close. "Everything will work out. I'll make sure of it."

He drove them into downtown Sonoma. He walked patiently beside her as she visited shop after shop, restaurant after restaurant. She talked to clerks, to managers, to waiters, to maître d's.

However, no one remembered seeing the nervous stranger.

But they did see Marissa Paige.

"Naomi!"

A frantic fluttering caught his eye just as his ear registered the familiar voice. Marissa sat at an outside table at a coffee shop, sipping coffee with her husband. As they approached, Mr. Paige glanced up from his newspaper and nodded to Naomi and Devon, then sank back in his seat to flip to the Sports section.

Devon blinked as he looked at the odd couple. Marissa's energy seemed to make her husband look only more calm and lethargic.

"Thank you so much for upgrading my facial yesterday, Naomi."

"My pleasure, Mrs. Paige."

"Would you be able to squeeze me in for a massage tomorrow?"

Naomi pulled out her cell phone. "I think my morning is booked, but if you wanted to arrive later, I could squeeze you in. Is seven o'clock too late?"

Marissa grimaced, but smiled. "Serves me right for not booking you sooner. That would be fine."

Naomi called the spa to set up Marissa's appointment, said their goodbyes, and continued down the sidewalk. However, Naomi seemed to be in a bigger hurry than before.

"Why the rush?"

"We have to get back to your car. We have to go to Papillon."

"Where?"

"The restaurant the Paiges were eating the night you were almost run down."

"Why?"

"I just remembered I was going to speak to the manager—he's a friend of my father's—about what he remembers about the Paiges that night. About who they might have talked to, who might have stolen Marissa's keys."

They drove to the French restaurant in only a few minutes, and within a few more, the manager had seated them at an empty table near the back with coffee and some delectable French pastries. Naomi dug into her napoleon with relish even as she listened to the manager talking about the Paiges.

"Such good customers," Adrien was saying. "They always come in once or twice when they visit Sonoma. Mr. Paige always has beef. Mrs. Paige orders whatever special is on the menu."

"I know it's hard to notice when the restaurant is busy, but did you see if the Paiges talked to anyone that night?" Naomi asked.

"Actually…" Adrien's neck had turned the color of cherries flambé. "There was a young woman Mrs. Paige argued with during dinner. It caused quite a stir."

"A woman?" Why hadn't Marissa mentioned that when they'd called on her? Although Devon supposed it wouldn't be something she'd want to confess to her massage therapist and a stranger.

"Long, straight blond hair, very slender." Adrien paused and rubbed the side of his nose. "She did not carry herself very elegantly."

Naomi's brow wrinkled. "What do you mean?"

Adrien sighed. "I try not to judge my customers. In fact, one of my best patrons always arrives in jeans and work boots—he owns a large vineyard in Geyserville. But this woman…" Adrien's eyes rolled, ever so slightly. "She chewed gum the entire time, except when she stuck it on the tablecloth in order to eat. She bellowed for a waiter whenever she wanted something—more water, or another drink, or to complain about her food. She said the salmon was *under-cooked*." Adrien sighed. "Her dinner companion was an older gentleman who never attempted to check her behavior."

"What happened with the woman and Mrs. Paige? Did Mrs. Paige approach her, or the other way around?" Devon asked.

"The woman was waiting for her dessert when she got up and approached the Paiges. Her behavior was actually quite familiar with Mrs. Paige. Mrs. Paige tried to ignore her, but the woman became more belligerent. Then they started a heated argument."

"Argument? About what?"

"I couldn't hear—thank goodness they weren't talking too loudly—but Mrs. Paige seemed to be accusing the woman of something."

"Accusing her? Did she know her?"

"It seemed like it. Eventually, the younger woman huffed back to her table, and she and her dinner companion left a few minutes later."

Had this been the woman who had stolen Marissa's car keys? Devon wondered.

"When did this happen—at the end of the Paiges' dinner?"

"No, they'd just ordered."

The timing was about right. The woman would have had

time to steal the keys and their car and head to Devon's hotel to lie in wait for him. His hotel didn't have its own restaurant, so most patrons walked next door to Alexander's Steak House—it would have been natural to assume Devon would walk across the parking lot to eat.

"Did anyone else speak to the Paiges that night?"

"If anyone did, I did not see it," Adrien replied.

"Did you get a name from the young woman's check when they paid?" Naomi asked.

Adrien thought a moment. "Perhaps. Wait here a moment."

Naomi sat fidgeting. "The timing fits."

"But one thing bothers me."

"What?"

"If she intended to steal the Paiges' car, why draw attention to herself by arguing with them?"

"She could have stolen the keys during the argument out of spite for Marissa Paige."

"And then ditched her boyfriend and used the car to try to run me over? She was a busy girl that night."

Naomi shrugged. "We don't have any other ideas about who stole the Paiges' car."

Adrien returned with a shake of his head. "The gentleman paid cash."

Devon looked in surprise at Naomi, whose eyebrows were also raised.

"Cash?" she said. "At Papillon?"

Adrien nodded. "It happens more often than you would think."

They gave Adrien heartfelt thanks and were about to leave when Naomi halted in her tracks and rummaged through her purse. "I almost forgot. Adrien, have you seen this man sometime this week?"

Adrien studied the picture of the stranger, but shook his head.

"Jessica Ortiz didn't come in this past week?" Devon asked.

"Who? I don't think I know her. At least, she's not a regular at Papillon."

"Well, thanks, Adrien."

They continued on their way out of the restaurant, which was already starting to fill with patrons for the busy lunch hour, when a voice hailed him. "Devon!"

Dr. Amir Dehlavi and his wife were sitting at a corner table. Devon veered to the side and shook his hand. "Good to see you, Amir. On vacation?"

"Yes, finally!" Mrs. Dehlavi stood to give him a hug. "You'd think he was the only one working in his office, the way he was going."

Devon smiled. "I'm glad he finally gave you a vacation, Mumtaz."

"The receptionist is always overlooked." She gave him a wink as she sat back down.

"This is Naomi Grant. She's head massage therapist at Joy Luck Life Spa, owned by her father, Augustus Grant."

"Nice to meet you, Naomi." Mumtaz's warmth radiated from her as strongly as her rampant curiosity. Her bright dark eyes flitted from Naomi to Devon and back again.

"Naomi, this is Amir and Mumtaz Dehlavi. Amir is a general practitioner—he and I know each other from medical school. Mumtaz is his receptionist."

"In case you hadn't gathered that already," Mumtaz said with a smile. "And he's finally taking me for a well-deserved vacation to Sonoma wine country."

"How long are you staying?"

"A week."

"Did you just finish lunch?" Amir asked.

"No, we were talking to the manager."

Amir's brow furrowed. "There's nothing to worry about, is there?"

"Oh, no," Naomi assured him. "He's a friend of my father's." She glanced down and seemed to realize she was still holding the stranger's picture, so she moved to slide it back into her purse.

But Mumtaz started when she saw the photo. "Amir, is that Bill?"

The photo was almost back in her purse, but Naomi whipped it out again. "Do you recognize this man?"

Amir and Mumtaz studied it. "That's Bill Avers," they said at the same time.

"You know him? Who is he? Where is he?" Naomi eagerly asked.

Amir hesitated, but Mumtaz plunged forward. "He's Amir's patient. He comes in for checkups regularly."

"Mumtaz, he's a patient." Amir glanced at Devon apologetically. "We can't say anything about him because of patient-client privilege."

But Mumtaz skewered him with a hard look and a sassy smile. "You can't say anything because you're his doctor. But I'm only a receptionist—I'm not even your nurse-assistant—so I'm free to say whatever I like about what he's told me in passing."

Naomi's eyes glittered. "What do you know about him?"

Mumtaz leaned toward them. "He always seems to have very wealthy girlfriends who buy him lots of very nice watches."

The muscle in Devon's jaw clenched. He'd wondered about the men's watches that showed up on Jessica's astronomical credit card statements when they'd still been married but having problems. Had she been dating Bill Avers even then?

"Do you know anything about his current girlfriend? When was the last time you saw him?"

Mumtaz thought a moment. "I think it was three months ago. Now stop frowning at me, Amir." She stabbed a finger at him. "He's obviously in trouble. You wouldn't want to harbor a criminal, would you?"

"You don't even know what he's done," Amir protested. He turned to Devon. "Before my wife says anything more—why are you looking for Bill?"

He explained about Jessica Ortiz's murder and Bill showing up that evening.

"You see?" Mumtaz told her husband. "He's in some sort of trouble. We should go straight to the police."

"Well, um…" Naomi's neck turned a rosy shade. "We're not actually supposed to have this picture."

Mumtaz waved the problem away with a beringed hand. "I'll tell the police you talked to us about the terrible events at your spa, and we thought we recognized your description of the man as Amir's patient."

Hope blossomed in Devon's chest. Finally, something the police could go on, rather than suspecting himself and Naomi. He handed them Detective Carter's business card. "This is the man you should call. We'd appreciate it if you'd talk to him."

"Naomi, you mentioned that you found Jessica in your massage room. Do the police suspect that you did it?" Mumtaz asked.

Naomi blinked at Mumtaz's blunt question, but she answered readily. "Much of the evidence is a bit pointed."

"Then, Amir, we definitely should talk to the police as

soon as possible." She touched her husband's hand where it rested on the table. "Especially if the police have no leads except this poor girl."

"Yes, yes, we'll call him today." Amir gave his wife an exasperated but indulgent smile.

"Thank you so much," Naomi said.

"Don't you worry." Mumtaz reached out to touch Naomi's arm.

"I only hope we can help," Amir said.

"I'm sure you will," Naomi replied. "This might be the lead the police have been waiting for." She gave a smile wider than any he'd seen on her since Jessica's murder. "Then my life can go back to normal."

How she wanted normal.

Normal meant peaceful days at the spa. No stress, no worry. No blood, no bodies. No feelings of failure, no weight of responsibilities.

Just Naomi, doing what she loved best—making people relax and feel better. Just Naomi, being who she loved being—a massage therapist, not the spa owner's daughter, who was smack dab in the middle of this horrible mess.

She finished escorting a client to the main women's lounge and passed Rachel chatting with Eloise Fischer in a hallway. Eloise must have just arrived, because she was clothed in a glorious red suit that matched the large ruby pendant at the hollow of her throat. A spa staff member, who had probably been escorting Eloise to the Tamarind Lounge, stood a few feet away, waiting patiently for them to finish their conversation.

Rachel had that exceptionally glazed look in her eyes—more spacey even than normal—which meant Eloise was again complaining about the skin products or whatever new mask she'd tried during a previous visit.

Naomi felt a bit guilty to be relieved that Eloise enjoyed going straight to the source—Rachel, dermatologist-in-residence. Naomi would have had a hard time just smiling politely, as Rachel did now, and ignoring Eloise's outrageous demands and complaints.

She passed them quickly, before Eloise could pause for breath and decide to accost Naomi as well.

Naomi needed to double-check her schedule for the rest of the day. She could do it on her computer in her office, but the entrance foyer was closer.

Sarah and Iona straightened in their seats as they saw her, but not guiltily. They'd been chatting with each other while manning the desk. "Iona, I need to borrow your computer. I want to see my schedule for the rest of today."

"No problem, Miss Grant." Iona stood and vacated her chair for Naomi. "We were actually about to try to find you. Did Eloise Fischer talk to you?"

"No."

"She wanted to change her massage therapist later this afternoon. She wanted you, but we told her you're booked solid."

Sarah motioned her head toward the door that led to the therapy rooms. "She said she would find you and talk to you." Both receptionists looked a bit pained.

Naomi sighed. "Let's look at the schedule."

She worried, at first, that she might have to schedule Eloise for her lunchtime break, but instead she switched Eloise with the client scheduled with Naomi at four o'clock, who hadn't asked specifically for her as her therapist.

Things ran smoothly until one o'clock, when Naomi

was about to eat a hurried lunch at her desk. Iona called, sounding frantic.

"Miss Grant, *Moya Hillman* is here."

Naomi could hear Aunt Becca's gentle tones in the background, then a loud outburst from the acclaimed starlet. "What's wrong?"

"She's insisting we schedule her for a massage right now." Iona's voice was a trembling whisper. "What should we do?"

One-third of the spa staff was scheduled to be out at lunch right now, which limited her choices. Naomi set her sandwich down. "I'll take her. Tell Ms. Itoh to escort her to the Anise Lounge." Hollywood star Moya Hillman didn't often come to Joy Luck Life, but when she did, it was always last minute.

As Naomi emptied her pockets, she let out a sigh of relief that few of the exclusive Saffron members had been at the spa in the past week. Moya was the first since the day of Jessica's murder, and no other Saffron members were scheduled until tomorrow. Since they paid the exorbitant membership fee and had access to the private lounges—more luxurious than the Tamarind Lounge— they required much more pampering and attention. And accommodation, which Moya always took advantage of.

Several hours later, Naomi was heading down a corridor toward the Tamarind Lounge to collect Eloise Fischer for her appointment when she smelled something metallic.

Hydrochloric acid ate a basketball-sized hole in her stomach. She thrust a hand against the wall to steady herself and clenched her belly.

No. It couldn't be blood.

She followed the horrifyingly familiar scent down another hallway, this one with the private lounges. Past the

Anise Lounge, its door closed, where Moya still sat. Past the Lemongrass and Sorrel Lounges, with their doors wide open.

The door to the Ginger Lounge was only cracked open.

Her breath came fast and shallow, making the edges of her vision blur. She was going to faint. She wanted Devon here with her.

She took a step forward, then another one.

She reached a hand out to ease the door open.

The smell wafted out at her, strong and sickening.

No. No. No. This couldn't be happening. Not again.

She caught a glimpse of a figure on the floor, then saw the blood.

She started screaming, and couldn't stop.

TWELVE

"Miss Grant."

Naomi turned to face Detective Carter, who had just finished questioning the staff while she pulled herself together. "I saw who it was. Eloise Fischer," she said.

The detective nodded, but his eyes seemed to be avoiding hers. Yet his demeanor didn't seem hard or accusing. Just determined to find the truth.

"Did you have an appointment with Ms. Fischer today?"

"At four."

"And when was the last time you spoke to her?"

"I was with her a few days ago, the day the spa reopened. I was in the Anise Lounge with her, personally apologizing for the, uh…incident with Jessica."

"Did you do that with all your clients?"

"Only the Tamarind members and Saffron members who were there that day. I spoke to some of them at their hotels the day after the…"

"Yes."

"But I didn't speak to Eloise—she wasn't at her hotel. So I talked to her when she came in for her rescheduled appointment."

"Did you speak to Ms. Fischer today?"

"No."

The detective's eyebrows—very light against his tanned skin—almost disappeared when he raised them. "One of your staff mentioned seeing you talking to her earlier today."

"No, that wasn't me. Well, the receptionists said Eloise had wanted to speak to me about rescheduling her massage therapist but when I saw her, she was speaking to Rachel. She never stopped me to talk to me."

"Ah." The detective scribbled in his notebook.

"And, Detective…" She paused. "I don't know if any of the staff told you, but Eloise Fischer had on a ruby pendant when she came into the spa."

He gave her a sharp look.

"And when I found her, I noticed that it was gone."

Just like Jessica.

Why would someone have killed Eloise for that pendant when Moya Hillman had been dripping in diamonds?

But Eloise had been in the Tamarind Lounge, and while that wasn't as populated as the main lounge, there were still women in it. Whereas Moya had been alone in the Anise Lounge, and the only people who would have seen her would have happened to be in the hallways. The Anise Lounge had its own locker room facilities attached, so she wouldn't even have gone to the women's restroom.

An officer exited the Ginger Lounge with a box of bagged items. Detective Carter stopped him. He pulled out a large clear plastic bag with a lamp base—heavy stone, smeared with blood.

She gagged and squeezed her eyes shut. After a moment, she could breathe again.

"I'm sorry, Miss Grant, but I have to ask you—is this lamp yours?"

She forced herself to look at it. "I've never seen it before. It doesn't belong to the spa. It's not the right decoration. It doesn't fit with the other pieces we bought for the lounges." Where had it come from? How could the killer have snuck it into the spa?

Well, it wasn't large. The lamp base was actually small enough for a client or a spa staff member to have brought it in, hidden in a large purse, she supposed.

As the officer dropped the lamp base back into the box, Naomi caught a glimpse of something pink. A very familiar pink.

Before the officer could move away, she leaned over to look inside the box and stared at the crumpled pink napkin from her favorite San José Victorian tea shop. With small circles of blood. Encased in an evidence bag.

"Where did you find that napkin?" she demanded.

"Miss Grant—"

"No, please answer me. Where did you find that?"

Detective Carter hesitated, then finally answered, "In Ms. Fischer's hand."

"No."

"Miss Grant?"

She tore her eyes away. "That napkin was in my office trash can. The night after Jessica was found."

She cast her mind back to that night—to Devon dabbing at his bleeding hand. "Don't you remember? We called you here after the stranger came by. He cut Devon Knightley's hand. I gave Devon that napkin. You saw it."

Detective Carter stared hard at the wall for a moment, then he replied, "Yes, I remember. He threw it in your office trash can."

"I think that's the same napkin. It's from a San José tea shop—three hours south of Sonoma. I went there a few weeks ago." She gestured forcefully at the bagged napkin in the box. "That will have Devon Knightley's blood on it."

But why had it been in Eloise Fischer's hand?

Had someone planted that napkin on Eloise? Anyone could have easily taken it from Naomi's trash can.

Especially since only a few days ago, she'd thought someone had rummaged through her office.

And whoever took the napkin would never have known the blood wasn't Naomi's.

Devon had gone back to his office and so he didn't hear about the second murder until Naomi called him late in the evening. What a day for him not to have been there for her.

He arrived early the next morning and met her at the spa as she'd asked him to.

She let him in the front door. Mauve half moons sagged under her eyes, and her hair, while neat, was limp. He reached for her, but she pulled away from him.

He understood, yet he felt as if she'd lashed out at him.

The entrance foyer echoed as they crossed to the receptionists' desk. Her step was sharp, purposeful. She punched into the keyboard with unnecessary force.

"The spa is closed?" He regretted the question as soon as he'd asked it. Of course it was closed after a murder. The empty parking lot, the lack of valets, the lack of therapists and aestheticians—all testaments to that fact.

She had paled, but her face remained impassive. "Dad went ballistic. He didn't want me to be here today."

"Why did you want to be here?"

"Because I can't just stand here and do nothing!" Her voice rang out in the empty foyer with a harsh echo.

She turned back to the computer. "I'm cross-checking the appointments to see who had been at the spa yesterday before two o'clock."

"Why two?"

"I heard someone—the coroner, I think—say that Eloise had been killed about two or three hours before. That puts her time of death before two o'clock."

She sounded so clinical, detached. As if women died in her spa every day of the week. "Naomi."

She looked up at him, but with a mouth firm and defiant, and eyes a bit wild. "Another woman died on my watch. And, Devon, whoever rifled through my office planted a napkin on—"

"Someone rifled through your office? When?" His jaw tightened reflexively.

She batted her hand in the air. "A few days ago. At least, I thought so, but I didn't have proof. But, Devon." She captured his attention with her burning gaze. "That bloody napkin. That stupid pink napkin was in Eloise's hand."

His gut tightened and burned at the same time. "The napkin with my blood on it."

"But don't you see? No one taking the napkin would have known the blood was yours. They would have assumed it was mine."

The burning in his gut ignited. "They planted it on Eloise's body?"

"I think so." She turned back to the computer. "Will you help me compare clients from yesterday and when Jessica was murdered?"

The overlapping clients were mercifully few—three.

"Keiko Uzaki was in a ninety-minute massage from twelve-thirty to two."

Devon checked her off the short list.

"Ron Hunt was in a massage and seaweed wrap from twelve to two."

Another check.

Suddenly Naomi stilled.

"Naomi?" he said.

"The only one left is Gloria Reynolds."

"Who is that?"

"I never told you—I talked to Eloise Fischer the day the spa reopened. She said that Jessica had argued with Gloria Reynolds the day she was killed. Gloria's a Tamarind member. I never got a chance to speak to her after Jessica's murder. Her personality is a bit cold. She gets facials, pedicures, manicures, but never massages."

"What does she do?"

"Actually…" She turned back to the computer. "I'm not sure."

They searched her name on the Internet, but there were too many results for Gloria Reynolds. "Narrow it to where she lives—San Francisco?"

"Sonoma." She inputted the search words. "There." She clicked on an article.

He read, "'Gloria Alexandra Reynolds visited Sakamoto High School yesterday to speak to the students about women in the workplace.'"

"Wait. Gloria *Alexandra?*"

He read it again. "Yes. So?"

"Do you remember what Jessica said? Before she died?" A name. "Andrea."

"What if she was saying 'Alexandra'?"

"But why would she call Gloria Reynolds by her middle name?"

"Well, she went by her full name for this press release. Maybe some people call her by her middle name."

It was a lead. What else did they have?

Naomi clicked on another article. "This one's better. Her husband is Donald Reynolds, and Gloria is vice president of sales for his company. He's in the diamond business."

Diamonds again. "My ex-wife was a lot of things, but she knew gemstones as well as any jeweler."

A small crease appeared between Naomi's brows. "I didn't know that. Maybe that's what Jessica argued with Gloria about." Naomi frowned deeply. "Eloise's ruby pendant was stolen yesterday."

"And Gloria Reynolds was at the spa the same day as both murders?" Devon asked.

"She had a facial at eleven, and she had a pedicure at two, so she would have been in the Tamarind Lounge in between her appointments."

"Or murdering Eloise Fischer."

"Devon, that's a little crass."

"I'm sorry."

Naomi studied a few more articles, then inhaled sharply. "What is it?"

She clicked onto a blog. The owner ranted about Donald Reynolds's shady business practices, hinting at criminal activity. As they continued searching, they saw more blogs. More accusations. More rumors.

Naomi sat back in the chair. "Several people have mentioned that the Reynoldses have some financial problems right now."

"But stealing necklaces? They wouldn't pay the mortgage on a house in San Francisco, much less bolster a diamond business."

"And Jessica's necklace wasn't especially valuable?"

"Aside from being expensive, it wasn't rare. My father

bought it from Tiffany's for my mother for an anniversary present. How about Eloise's pendant?"

She shook her head. "I don't know."

"Maybe the necklaces are red herrings. Maybe the intent was to kill Jessica and Eloise."

"But they weren't even friends. Eloise knew Jessica's mother—that's it—and from the way she said it, I don't think they were particularly good friends. Eloise liked to embellish the truth to make herself look more important."

"There has to be a connection between them."

She gestured to a photo on the computer screen. "Gloria Reynolds."

"Do you think she knew Eloise Fischer?"

"I'm sure she knew her—they were both Tamarind members—but know her well? I don't know."

He sighed. Too many tenuous connections, nothing solid. Nothing that led anywhere.

Naomi closed her eyes, took a deep breath. He watched her face as the lines around her mouth smoothed a little.

"Dear Jesus, please help us."

He'd never heard her pray before. It surprised him, but it also fueled his frustration. What had God done but make things worse and worse for her?

Her eyes were still closed, and she spoke as if she'd read his mind. "Aunt Becca is saying to just trust God, that He's got everything under His control. But I can't help thinking…" Her voice caught. She pressed her lips together.

Where was God?

She opened her eyes and straightened her back at the same time. "I'm tired of being afraid. I need to take charge of what's happening. Let's go find Gloria Reynolds."

THIRTEEN

"What do you mean, let *you* take the lead?" Naomi's eyes spit nails at Devon.

They paused a few feet from the front door of the Reynoldses' Sonoma home, shaded by a pompous portico. He kept his voice pitched low. "I know you're the spa owner's daughter—"

"Which is exactly why I should be the one talking, not you. Gloria doesn't even know you."

"Exactly."

"What do you mean by that?"

"She obviously knows you quite well. She *supposedly* doesn't know me. There's still a chance she's involved in those attacks on me."

Naomi shook her head, but there was less belligerence in her tone when she answered him. "There's still no proof about the connection between Jessica and the attempts on your life. Especially now that Eloise has been killed—you didn't know her at all."

"It's simple. If Gloria doesn't know me, she shouldn't react differently when she sees me for the first time. If she does react, I'll know she's involved in the attacks on me, and it'll be easy to just make an excuse and get us out of the house."

"That's assuming she answers her front door. She could have a butler or a maid."

He shrugged. "I'll come up with some other story so that we can see her—but she's going to see me before she sees you."

"Well, once we're inside—"

"You're still going to let me take the lead."

"No."

"Yes."

She made an exasperated noise. "This is ridiculous. Why wouldn't I talk to Gloria?"

"Your taking over the spa is relatively recent. Do you really think she's going to see you as anyone besides a massage therapist?"

"My father owns that spa," she said through teeth gritted in frustration.

"And Jessica was one of your dedicated clients, and Gloria had an argument with her. Do you think she's going to confess to you what she argued about? Wouldn't she be more likely to be lulled into telling me, a stranger?"

"Assuming she doesn't know you."

"That'll be easy to find out."

"She might be a good actress."

"Not that good, if she was dumb enough to argue publicly with a woman she was going to murder."

Naomi's mouth pinched, but she didn't respond to his logic.

He'd made a career out of skillfully reading patients' body language. If he didn't know the truth behind an injury, or the extent of someone's pain, he might make a bad decision. He was confident he'd at least be able to know if Gloria Reynolds recognized him or not.

And, not to be arrogant, but he was reasonably sure he could charm Gloria Reynolds more than Naomi could, given her present state of nervous stress.

They knocked on the door, which was answered by a short, stout Hispanic woman. Her dour expression didn't bode well, so he adopted a calm, professional demeanor. "Good morning. May we please speak with Mrs. Gloria Reynolds?"

"Who is calling?"

"Augustus Grant sent us." He could sense Naomi fuming beside him, but he ignored her. He didn't want to mention Naomi, but he also didn't want to mention his own name before Gloria saw him.

"I will see if she is available."

He placed a hand against the closing door. "May we come inside while we wait?"

The maid hesitated, then opened the door wider. "Please wait in the foyer."

The house had magnificent proportions and excellent echoes. He heard light, snappy footsteps from the luxurious rooms to his right even before the servant headed in that direction to intercept her employer.

The room was a parlor, richly furnished, with a doorway leading off it from the far side. When Gloria Reynolds entered, he had a clear view of her, and vice versa.

Her eyes flickered over him—appreciative of his figure and demeanor, he could tell, but no recognition. She shifted to Naomi, and the eyes cooled a fraction.

He'd been right to insist on taking the lead. Naomi didn't trigger any good associations with Gloria, considering the two murders in the spa within the past week.

"Hello, Mrs. Reynolds. I am Dr. Devon Knightley, and you know Miss Grant." He walked forward, hand extended, his footsteps sinking into muted silence in the luxurious rug on the hardwood floor.

She took his hand coolly, automatically. This wasn't a woman to be charmed by a handsome face, and he certainly wasn't a movie star. "Do I know you?" she asked.

"I'm a colleague of Augustus Grant."

Her smile warmed slightly. She was an informed businesswoman, then. Because even though Joy Luck Life was a service-oriented business, it was also common knowledge that, in combination with risky but intelligent investments and keen business savvy, Augustus grossed more than most high-tech industries in this area, and his name carried weight as well as respect.

"As you know, Augustus has been recovering from a small stroke the past few months."

"Yes. We were very sorry to hear that." Gloria gestured for them to be seated in one of the stiff, stuffy chairs in the parlor. Devon recognized what type of room this was. This was a place she left her husband's business associates to cool their heels, a place she entertained women from clubs and groups whom she didn't like but wanted to impress, a place for visits lasting only fifteen minutes or, at most, half an hour.

He needed her to forget her surroundings so she'd show a crack in her armor. "We are here as his representatives to personally apologize for the events that have transpired in the past week at the spa, and to reassure you that these matters are being dealt with by the police."

Gloria handled the situation with cool elegance. "Yes, such shocking events." She said it in the same manner she would if she were making a restaurant reservation.

"I understand you knew Eloise Fischer. You must have been terribly upset." He pitched his concern mildly, not too much charm.

She responded as he'd hoped—falling into his conversational gambit. "We knew each other in passing, but not well."

"Oh? Other Tamarind members mentioned that you were friends."

Confusion clouded her eyes. "No, not friends."

"Ah. I must have mistaken Eloise Fischer for Jessica Ortiz. You were friends with Jessica instead?"

At the name, color glowed in her cheeks. "Jessica Ortiz? I wasn't especially close to her, either."

"You didn't do business with her? Jessica Ortiz was known to be an expert in gemstones, especially diamonds." That was stretching the truth a bit—he didn't know if anyone else fully knew about Jessica's taste, knowledge and instinct.

A spasm passed across Gloria's throat.

He had her full attention now. No side glances to Naomi. All her energy was focused on the lie he'd caught her in, on hiding from him what he wanted to pull out of her. "Perhaps it was your husband who did business with Ms. Ortiz, then."

Distaste flickered across her face, and then was gone. "Perhaps."

Apparently, Mr. Reynolds disliked Jessica more than Gloria did. Devon wondered why. Had Jessica said or done something to jeopardize his business?

"Not to speak ill of the dead, but I had always thought Jessica Ortiz was prejudiced against your husband for some reason," Devon said.

She jumped on it. "She was. Spreading lies about his gemstones for no reason whatsoever, demanding her money back. Don't give any credence to what you've heard. He is still one of the finest judges of diamonds on the West Coast."

"Of course. Why would anyone pay attention to a flighty woman like that? After all, between your husband and Ms. Ortiz, there's no question about whom people would believe."

Her shoulders never truly relaxed, but the silk of her blouse eased into softer folds as she sat back. "And who did you hear these rumors from?"

"Other Tamarind members." He hoped Naomi would forgive him for maligning the spa's clients.

Gloria sniffed. "They're silly housewives who haven't the ability to even understand their husbands' businesses."

"Eloise Fischer did put on airs, I understand."

"That woman couldn't find her way out of a lighted room. Although…" She collected herself. "I do feel sorry for her family. She was apparently a kind mother to her children, from what I understand."

"Do you know her family well?"

"Oh no, I hardly knew her at all. I could barely stand chatting with her."

Her facial expressions and body language told him she wasn't lying. She really hadn't known Eloise Fischer well. "Ms. Fischer never inquired about your husband's jewels? I thought she supposedly had an extensive collection."

"Eloise Fischer? Her only valuable stone was a ruby pendant, and even that was hardly mentionable." She eyed him, a bit like a hawk who was trying to decide what to do about a rat. "You listen to a great deal of rumor, Dr. Knightley."

He pasted on a neutral smile and spread his hands wide. "I hear too many things in my profession and in my association with Augustus, especially about the businesses of notable business owners."

The lines around Gloria's mouth lengthened subtly, although she was trying to keep her expression still.

"I apologize, Mrs. Reynolds. I shouldn't listen to rumors," he said.

"There's no truth in any of it," she replied, a bit too quickly.

"Of course not. Donald Reynolds has a history of making strong decisions."

She smiled stiffly.

"Is your husband much acquainted with Augustus Grant?" It was a long shot, but there wasn't much else he could milk out of this verbal sparring.

To his surprise, Gloria gave a wider smile than she had since they'd entered her house. "We are not as closely acquainted as we'd like to be." It seemed that she suddenly remembered Naomi's silent presence, for she turned to her with that same unctuous smile. "We would love to invite your family to dinner at some point, Miss Grant."

"Thank you, Mrs. Reynolds." Her voice could have been drizzled on a cinnamon roll. "I'm afraid we don't understand the diamond industry very well, however. We are woefully uninformed."

Gloria gave a short, light laugh. "We wouldn't invite you over to discuss business. We'd love to simply get to know you all."

Stranger and stranger. Naomi's eyes met his with a wild confusion behind them, although she kept her expression firmly polite.

"We've already taken up too much of your time, Mrs. Reynolds." He rose to his feet. Naomi followed suit, hastily.

"Thank you for stopping by." Gloria spoke more to Naomi than to Devon. "And please let me know when would be a good day for your family to come by."

"With three sisters, our schedules are often very disparate."

"Well, I must say I'm especially interested in getting to know your sister Rachel much better. I believe I met her briefly at the Fireman's Ball this past year."

Naomi's smile hardened. "Yes, she might have mentioned that."

They said their goodbyes and as soon as the front door shut behind them, Naomi hightailed it to his car, leaving a cloud of dust in her wake.

"Slow down. What's wrong?"

"She's never met Rachel. We don't go to the Fireman's Ball."

"Maybe she was mistaken."

"Rachel is the real reason she suddenly changed tactics in the conversation. What could Gloria want with her?"

"Do facial products have anything to do with diamonds?" Devon asked.

Naomi's step stuttered. "Diamonds." Her face had gone white.

"What is it?"

"Rachel was working on top-secret formulations. Some involved carbon-based minerals."

"Diamonds."

"But Devon," she said, grabbing his shirtsleeve. "No one is supposed to know about Rachel's research. How would Gloria Reynolds know, unless…" She swallowed. "Unless she's spying on the spa?"

FOURTEEN

"None of this adds up." Naomi bit into a slice of cheese as she surveyed the wonderful view.

They'd bought cheese, salami and fruit and driven to Lake Sonoma Winery, high in the foothills and several minutes north of Sonoma at the end of a winding road. The countryside spread out before them as they sat on the winery's outside patio and ate their lunch.

Naomi had suggested coming here. She loved this view, and after the undercurrents of tension and secrets from the interview with Gloria Reynolds, she needed to be here, to let the cool breeze fill her lungs and remove the shadows within her.

"Gloria did know Jessica," Devon said, popping a grape in his mouth.

"And apparently Jessica said something disparaging about her husband's diamonds. Perhaps there's some truth to the rumor that he's selling poor-quality stones."

"Jessica would have been able to tell poor quality. She knew her jewels."

"Perhaps that's what they argued about."

"But is that enough for Gloria to want to kill her?"

"I don't know." Naomi sat back in her patio chair.

"Gloria also didn't know Eloise Fischer. I'm not one hundred percent certain, but I do believe she was telling the truth there."

"That leaves us with nothing."

"And why take the necklaces? Jessica's—rather, my mother's necklace—wasn't from Donald Reynolds. And from what Gloria said, she didn't think much of Eloise's pendant, so it was unlikely that was from her husband's business, either."

Naomi shook her head. "My instincts are telling me that the necklaces are a ruse. The real motive was getting rid of Jessica and Eloise."

"Not to discount your instincts, but we don't have proof of that. And to most people, those necklaces are still worth a great deal of money."

"And there's truth in the rumors that the Reynoldses' business isn't doing very well, but they're desperately trying to hide it."

"Well, wouldn't you find it embarrassing?"

"Yes, I would. I almost feel sorry for her," Naomi said.

"Maybe she really does have nothing to do with the two murders. She didn't know who I was today—not when she saw me, and not when she heard my name."

"Or maybe the attacks against you are completely separate from the murders. Who have you upset lately?"

Devon sighed and sat back in his chair, frustration clouding his face. "That's just it. I don't know."

They sat in silence for a while. Naomi watched a hawk lazily circling in the sky. The conversation with Gloria today had been ultimately unproductive. What did they get out of it except more questions and more loose ends that seemed to lead nowhere?

Her cell phone chirped. She checked the caller ID but didn't recognize the number. "Hello?"

"Naomi Grant?" asked a gruff voice, with underlying oiliness making his words slick and hard to follow.

She hesitated. Something told her not to answer him, not to confirm it.

"It's too late to try hiding, Miss Grant. I want my money."

"I don't know what you're talking about."

"If you play, you have to pay up. That's what I told you when you came to me."

"Who is this? I've never met you."

Devon had straightened in his chair. "Who is that? What's wrong?" he whispered.

"I hate liars as much as I hate thieves. And you're a thief. Bet you didn't think I'd find this number," the man on the phone said.

Her heart was pounding slow, hard, painfully against her chest. "I haven't stolen anything from you."

"Ten thousand dollars ain't nothing. I'm not a patient man."

"Ten thousand dollars?"

"I want my money, or your pretty sisters will be strung up by their thumbs."

"You've got the wrong number."

"You've got three days." Click.

She dropped her cell phone, and a few pieces flew as it fell against the floor. Her heart throbbed as if a knife plunged into her with each beat. She gasped. She couldn't breathe.

"Naomi!" Devon's face swam in front of her. "What happened?"

"Someone…some man. Saying I stole money from him."

"What?"

"Ten thousand dollars. I didn't understand what he was saying."

"Maybe he got the wrong number."

"He called me by name." She closed her eyes and clenched her chest. *Oh, God. God, where are You?*

How could she believe in God's strength and sovereignty? He could rip apart this net closing around her. Why didn't He do it? Why was He forsaking her?

My God, my God, why have You forsaken me?

Suddenly she was sobbing, her face pressed against Devon's shoulder. Why wouldn't God help her? Why wouldn't He shine light in this darkness all around her? She was so afraid, and He wasn't doing anything to help her, to let her know He was still there.

And surely I am with you always, to the very end of the age.

Then why wouldn't God show Himself?

It hurt to pray. It hurt her heart. It hurt her spirit.

The Lord your God is with you, He is mighty to save.

No. No, He wasn't. He hadn't, not yet.

Those who hope in the Lord will renew their strength. They will soar on wings like eagles.

She remembered the hawk, its slow, patient circles. She wasn't patient. Time was running out—she could sense it.

The Lord your God is with you, He is mighty to save.

"Oh God," she whispered. "Where are You?"

Devon held Naomi as if his arms were the only thing keeping her from shattering. Maybe it was true.

He sensed that something deeper was going on inside her. Something more than the phone call, something harder for her to take. He wondered if her faith always stayed strong and solid, the way it seemed to with her family. Where was God now?

Who are you to question her faith? You have none.

But a part of him wondered. A part of him wanted to have faith.

And a part of him just wanted to rebel against his opinionated, atheist father. He had to admit that.

Maybe when this was over, he could ask her about her faith. Maybe he could talk to her aunt.

And maybe her faith wouldn't survive this.

What was he thinking? Who was he to doubt her? Faith had carried countless thousands of Christians through hard times, grief, loss.

Except that he only cared about this one Christian. And wished he could do something, anything, to help her.

And that's when he knew he was falling in love with her.

She quieted and pulled away. She wiped her eyes, then vainly wiped at his damp shirt.

"What happened? How can I help you?" he asked.

She hiccuped. "I'm not even sure what happened. A man called. He knew my name. Said I owed him ten thousand dollars."

"Who was it?"

She shook her head, and tears sprayed from her eyes. "I don't know."

"What did he say?"

"That if I didn't get him the money in three days, he'd hurt my sisters."

He picked up her phone from the floor. Pieces were broken off, but the screen lighted when he pressed a button. He jotted down the caller's phone number.

He pulled out his own cell phone.

"Who are you calling?"

"Detective Carter."

"Again? He's going to think—"

"What he'd better think is that someone is trying to hurt you, and that he'd better do something about it." Devon punched "send" on his phone.

"Detective Carter."

"It's Devon Knightley."

"What can I do—"

"Naomi Grant just got a call from a man who says she owes him ten thousand dollars." Suddenly, hearing himself say it, he wondered if this might be hurting Naomi, rather than helping the case. He almost shut his phone.

"A man? Who?"

"He didn't say. Here's the caller ID number." He rattled it off.

"I don't recognize it. I'll cross-reference it."

"He threatened her."

"What exactly did he say?"

Devon looked into Naomi's wide eyes, bright and wet. "What exactly did he say?"

She stared at the ground as she thought. "I don't recall exactly…I was so upset. Something about…he'd string my sisters up by their thumbs. Something weird like that."

Devon repeated it to Detective Carter, but received only silence in reply. "Detective?"

"She's certain that's what he said?"

"Yes."

The detective sighed. "I know who she spoke to," he said.

"What? Who?"

"A bookie. Dusty Price. He's been suspected of some unusual murders in the past year."

"Unusual?"

"Victims strung up by their thumbs and wrists. It's a form of crucifixion—they suffocate slowly. We've never caught him. Never proved it was him."

"Devon, what is it?" Naomi touched his forearm. Her eyes were frightened. She looked the way he felt.

"He's a very dangerous man, Dr. Knightley." Detective Carter sighed again. "Protect Miss Grant. You've got to protect her."

"We never asked Gloria about her middle name," Naomi said to Devon the following day as they sat in the outdoor seating area of a café in downtown Sonoma.

"Gloria just makes the entire thing more convoluted and confusing."

She and Devon had stopped for lunch after Naomi had done her duty this morning and made calls on the Tamarind members who had been at the spa when Eloise's body was discovered. A few clients had already left town, but she had managed to appease a few with her personal attention and promises of pampering attention when they rescheduled.

If the spa ever opened again. But she didn't tell them that.

They'd also stopped by the mobile phone store to get her a new phone. Transferring her SIM card had been quick and easy, and her broken phone sat in her purse alongside her new one.

The thought of the phone made her deliberately shift her mind away from the memory of the bookie's call yesterday. Devon had told her what Detective Carter had said, and the stress and worry had been eating at her insides all morning during her calls to the spa's clients.

"How dare you!" The shrill voice that distracted Naomi's attention was familiar to her.

She craned her neck around a family of four who was noisily passing their table. Across the street, in front of a pottery shop, she saw Marissa Paige.

And a young woman with long, straight blond hair.

"Devon!" she exclaimed, excitedly.

"I see them." He rose and tossed a few bills on the table. "Let's get closer."

Marissa seemed so upset she'd forgotten her surroundings, Naomi realized. Her entire being raged at the pouting blond woman in a silky sundress.

"You're an animal!" Marissa shouted. "You hunt down innocent men and devour them."

"Your pansy son would be devoured by a bunny rabbit," the woman sneered.

"Don't you talk that way about him!" Marissa lunged.

Devon sprinted the few feet that separated them and grabbed Marissa's arms while the young woman teetered backward on her expensive heels.

Marissa beat against him with flailing arms. "Let me go! She's a tramp!"

"Mrs. Paige." Devon spoke low but firmly. "That might be true, but you're not behaving like a lady."

Marissa collapsed against him in a flurry of tears.

The blonde gave her a disdainful stare. "Psychotic, overprotective…"

"You'd better leave," Naomi said, stepping into her line of vision.

The blonde's pink mouth squeezed into a lemon-drop shape. "She's the one who won't leave me alone—"

"No, you're the one trying to upset her." Naomi pointed to the shopping bags discarded at Marissa's feet, then to an older gentleman sitting on a bench several yards away, watching the scene with a bored expression. "She was out shopping and you went out of your way to make sure she saw you. What are you trying to do, pick a fight?" Naomi stood up straighter and rolled her shoulders in what she hoped was an intimidating gesture.

The blonde turned her nose up and stalked away.

Naomi went back to where Marissa stood, swiping at her blotchy eyes while Devon picked up her fallen shopping bags.

"Mrs. Paige, where's your husband?"

"He's having lunch with some business partners." She sniffled. "I was just doing some shopping…" Her voice cracked.

"Let's get you something to drink." They escorted her across the street back to the café where they'd been eating.

Devon spoke to a waiter, who sat them immediately at a table in a dark corner. Naomi took Marissa to the women's restroom.

Mrs. Paige wiped her face and fixed her makeup in silence. But as she was reapplying her lipstick, tears filled her eyes again, and she bowed her head.

Naomi took tissues from a nearby box and put them in Marissa's hand.

"Thank you," she said, her voice muffled in the tissues. "Did that woman…"

"She's my son's ex-girlfriend." Marissa started sobbing again. "She hurt him horribly. Then I said things about her to my friends that ruined her relationship with another young man even wealthier than our son."

"So she's upset with you?"

"She seems to enjoy following me, making a spectacle of herself, embarrassing me, needling me with her comments. I've tried so hard to ignore her…"

And today she'd cracked.

Marissa again fixed her makeup. When they returned to the table, Devon had ordered some ice water for them both.

"Naomi, Detective Carter called." Devon's words were light enough, but he said them slowly.

"And?"

"He needs to speak to you. He should be here in a few minutes." A crease between his brows deepened as he spoke.

"What's wrong?"

Devon hesitated before answering. "I'm not sure. Something seemed…off."

They sat mostly in silence. Marissa sighed a great deal as she sipped her water. She also attempted to smile at Naomi and Devon to convey her thanks that they had stayed to take care of her.

In a few minutes, Detective Carter entered the café—followed by two policemen. Patrons turned to look at the odd procession.

Something in Naomi's gut did a quick flip.

"Miss Grant." Detective Carter removed his sunglasses, but he didn't look directly at her. He wasn't as confident as he usually was—he seemed almost unsure of what he was doing. "Would you please come with us?"

Her hands started to shake, while at the same time, they became completely numb, as if she'd plunged them into buckets of ice water. She stood and swayed on her feet because she couldn't seem to feel them, either. "What is it?"

Devon also stood. "What's going on?"

"Miss Grant, I need you to come with us."

A policeman moved to stand behind her. She wanted to step away from him, but she couldn't move—her feet wouldn't respond.

Then the policeman grabbed her wrists—and hand-cuffed her.

She stared at the detective's face, willing him to look at her, willing that grim look to melt from his face. *Please, God. Please help me…*

"Detective Carter?" A plea. A sob sounded behind her words.

He took a deep breath, and then finally looked at her. His eyes were both hard and sad at the same time.

"Naomi Grant, you're under arrest for the murder of Eloise Fischer."

FIFTEEN

The drive to the station was both short and long at the same time. She kept her eyes squeezed shut, hoping none of the people she knew in Sonoma would recognize her in the back of the squad car.

She felt completely broken.

She tried to boost her spirits with the thought that her family would soon arrive at the police station to help her out—as she was being led away, Devon had said he'd follow her, but she'd instructed him to instead get her aunt and bring her with him.

The officers escorted her into the police station. She took her first few steps with her head down, mortified and terrified.

But…what was she doing? She wasn't guilty.

She wasn't going to walk into the building as if she were.

She tossed her head back so hard, her neck cracked. She set her eyes ahead of her, walking like a blind woman. Except she wasn't blind enough not to see the man walking out of the front doors.

He was nervous. Really nervous. He had light eyes. Light blond hair. Light build.

"That's Bill Avers!" she screeched. "Why are you letting him go? Detective, you're letting him go." She whipped around to look at Detective Carter, walking behind her.

"Miss Grant—"

"Why are you letting him go? He's the guy who came to the spa looking for Jessica Ortiz. He ran when he realized something was wrong. Why are you letting him go?"

"Miss Grant—"

"You have to tell me. You're arresting me, but you're letting him go. You have to tell me." Random people around her turned to stare. She didn't care. Her life was falling apart around her.

"Miss Grant." Detective Carter sighed. "He has an alibi for both murders."

All sound faded to a low-pitched buzzing. In slow motion, she saw Bill Avers scurry past her to the parking lot, avoiding her eye. Escaping. Escaping.

They processed her and took her to a windowless room, seating her at an empty table. In a few minutes, Detective Carter came in and removed her handcuffs. He avoided looking her straight in the eye, and she studied a tic in his jaw.

She started to suspect that he didn't want to do this.

It didn't ease the turmoil inside her, but it was a chink of light.

"This is a nightmare." She stared at the scarred tabletop.

Detective Carter didn't say anything at first. Finally, he pushed a piece of paper toward her. "Miss Grant, is this your credit card number?"

She had to read it three times because the numbers kept swimming in front of her eyes. "I think so." She'd need her wallet to be certain, but she bought so many things online and had to type in her number, she was fairly sure it was hers.

"Did you purchase this lamp online with your credit card at 10:02 p.m. five days ago?" From a box at his feet, he pulled out the stone lamp base that had been used to kill Eloise Fischer. It was still in its evidence bag, still smeared with blood.

"No! No, of course I didn't buy that."

"You didn't buy this lamp?"

"No."

The detective sighed. "You didn't have it sent to the spa?"

"What? No."

"You didn't receive a package two days ago? We have the UPS tracking number that indicates it was delivered that morning."

"No, I haven't received any packages in a week at least. Shipping and Receiving never told me I had a package."

It was delivered to the spa.

Someone had retrieved it from Receiving.

It was now obvious that whoever had ordered it was a spa staff member.

Her entire body shuddered, and she couldn't stop.

"Miss Grant?"

"It's one of my staff."

"Miss Grant—"

"Someone rifled through my office five days ago."

The detective gave her a look as if to say, *Too little, too late.*

"No, I'm serious. I didn't have proof, so I never reported it. But you can ask my sister Rachel. She was there. I forgot to lock my desk, and my purse was in the drawer."

"Who has access to your office?" He sounded as if he were just humoring her.

"Anyone. Anyone."

"So you're saying…?"

"Someone could have stolen my credit card number and the security code on the back and purchased that lamp online."

"It's a handy coincidence that your office was rifled through."

"I'm not making this up. Could you find the ISP address of the computer that bought that lamp? Did you trace it to my computer? I'm guessing you didn't. Because I didn't buy it."

The detective removed the lamp and put it back in the box. "Miss Grant, can you account for your whereabouts between one and two o'clock on the day of Eloise Fischer's murder?"

"Yes," she said, straightening. "Yes, I can. I took a last-minute appointment."

"You don't have an appointment in the schedule we copied from the spa's reservation computer," he said.

"It was last minute. Iona was manning the desk—she'll remember. Moya Hillman arrived and demanded a massage. I skipped lunch to take her. Ask Aunt Becca— she was at the desk, too. Ask Moya."

Detective Carter was scribbling in his notebook furiously. "You're certain of the time?"

"Yes. Ask Iona and Aunt Becca. They put Moya in the Anise Lounge. I collected her a few minutes later. I had her until a little after two o'clock. And then I was busy with other clients until four o'clock." When she'd found Eloise. "Their names will be in the schedule."

She hadn't realized her chest had been so tight until it started loosening. Suddenly she could breathe more freely.

She had an alibi for the murder.

She had an alibi.

But then…who killed Eloise?

And why would they want to frame Naomi?

Twenty-four hours later she was free.

Even the air smelled tainted after her overnight stay in jail. It had been the most terrible, the most angry twenty-four hours Naomi had ever had, being forced to remain imprisoned despite knowing she had an alibi for the murder. The police had either had a hard time tracking Moya Hillman down to verify Naomi's alibi or they'd decided to keep her overnight simply because they had already arrested her and wanted to keep her in custody just in case they found other evidence against her.

The district attorney's office had refused to press charges because she'd had three different people confirm her alibi. Regardless, her father and Aunt Becca had been livid, especially Aunt Becca, since she had been at the station harassing every man or woman in a uniform from the moment she'd heard that Naomi had been arrested. She gave Detective Carter a decidedly icy stare when she escorted her niece out of the station.

Naomi still couldn't prove that someone had gone through her office and stolen her credit card number. But the credit card and the package shipped to her name at the spa's address involved her somehow with two murders.

Her world had been upended. She'd been arrested. She was still under suspicion.

One of her staff was trying to frame her.

Devon had accompanied Aunt Becca and Monica when they picked her up from the police station. He enveloped her in a hug that tried to squeeze the shadow of her jail experience out of her bones.

But on the road, she leaned forward from her seat in back. "I need to go to the spa."

"What?"

"What are you talking about?"

"Why?" asked Monica, calmer than the other two.

"If the murderer is one of the staff, I need to look at the background checks Dad had done for each of the staff before they were hired. They're at the spa."

"Dad had background checks done?" Monica turned in the front passenger seat to look at Naomi.

Aunt Becca, however, was nodding sagely. "That's a good idea. Devon, take us to the spa."

"Do you think it's safe?" he asked even as he flipped on his turning signal.

"The security guards are there. I would hope so."

"And so far, you're the only one who's been attacked," Monica told him reasonably. "The murderer is trying to frame Naomi, not kill her."

The spa looked peaceful and elegant in the bright sunlight as they drove up. Aunt Becca unlocked the front door rather than the back one, and they walked inside. Devon led the way to Naomi's office.

Naomi smelled the scent a few feet from the office. Eucalyptus. Very, very strong. As if an entire bottle had been poured out.

Devon's step slowed as he smelled it, too. Because he led the way, he reached the office doorway first and halted a moment, blocking the rest of them. Then he whipped around. "Wait in the foyer."

"What?"

"What's going on?" Monica tried to push past him.

"Don't go in there." His eyes had strain lines at the edges, and his mouth was grim and tight.

Naomi knew she should feel something—shock, anger, sadness. But she felt nothing. "Let me see."

"No—"

But she slipped under his arm and entered her office.

Eucalyptus slapped her in the face as she stepped inside. Everything was overturned. Papers strewn everywhere. The filing cabinet drawers open and empty. The contents of her desk all over the floor, her chair. The shelves swept clear of statues and knickknacks. Candles and broken aromatherapy bottles at the base of a small table. That's where the eucalyptus smell came from.

She could hear Aunt Becca hyperventilating behind her. She turned to see her aunt, as white as snow, shaking. "Monica."

Her sister pulled her shocked eyes away from the destruction, saw her aunt, and immediately ushered her out of the office. "Naomi—first aid kit?"

"In any of the therapy rooms. They should have whatever you need for shock."

Naomi said it so matter-of-factly. So calmly.

No, not calmly. She wasn't calm, exactly. She was stony. A thread of rage simmered below the surface. She took in the office with a certain dissociated observation. But calm? No. She wasn't calm.

She wanted to say, *This isn't happening,* but a small flare deep inside cut the words off at her tongue. She was past denial, past the need to speak words to try to reverse the present.

"This proves it was a staff member. No one else could get into the building." She turned to Devon, whose eyes bored into hers like embers. She knew he was trying to find her, to find the Naomi he knew under this granite stranger. But that Naomi had hidden herself away.

She moved through the mess, toward the locked filing cabinet in the far corner. The lock had been destroyed, the drawer hanging open crookedly. Papers had been tossed out, but most of the ones from that drawer were lying nearby.

Except the background checks.

She sifted through the papers on the floor. Paycheck information for the staff, private information on the clients.

No background checks. They were completely missing, conspicuous in itself.

"Call Detective Carter. I'm going to the security room."

"I'm going with you," he said as he pulled out his cell phone.

They found David and Neal manning the security desk. "Hello, Miss Grant."

"Have you watched the security cameras all morning?"

"Yes. No one came in before you did."

"We need to check the cameras now, and quickly. Dr. Knightley has called the police, and we'll need to turn over the video to them. But before we do, I want to find out who was in the spa last."

She sat in a chair. "Check the back-door video first. Where the staff come in."

Sure enough, they only had to backtrack a few hours to find the murderer who had entered the spa late last night. The hooded figure was hard to see because she kept to the shadows and moved slowly. If they hadn't been looking for her, they wouldn't have seen her.

It was most definitely a woman and she most definitely used a key to open the back door.

"Miss Grant," David whispered. "She used a staff key."

"I know."

The woman on the video left an hour later. If she carried

anything with her, it was hidden under her hooded sweat-shirt.

They never caught a glimpse of her face.

"She didn't park in the parking lot," Devon remarked as they watched her walk off camera.

"She probably parked her car along the highway and walked to the spa so the video wouldn't catch her car." Smart girl. But then again, she had to be to have killed two women. "I still don't know what she wants. Nothing adds up."

"Miss Grant, Detective Carter's at the front door," David said.

The look in the detective's eye was unreadable. But Naomi couldn't help remarking acerbically as she handed over the videos, "I hope you put more effort into catching whoever did this than you did in arresting me."

The muscle in his jaw flexed, but he didn't reply.

She didn't care. She'd been arrested—booked, finger-printed, photographed, searched. She'd spent the night in a jail cell, one of the most horrific experiences of her life.

No, she wouldn't think about it. She was amazed at how quickly she could shift her mind away from that experi-ence, but then again, she was no longer the Naomi from a few days ago. She felt nothing now. She heard nothing.

Not even God.

SIXTEEN

"Why did God let this happen to me, Poppa?" She hadn't called him that since she was a little girl. Her sisters and Aunt Becca had been in the living room with them for a while, but he must have somehow communicated that he wanted to be alone with her, because they'd left silently a few minutes ago.

He shook his head. "'The Lord your God is with you, He is mighty to save.'"

She'd remembered that verse earlier. Days ago. Years ago. "He's not, Poppa."

"'The Lord your God is with you, He is mighty to save.'"

"I wish He'd save me soon."

The silence in the room wore between them for a few minutes. Finally he said, "I don't know why, but all I can think about this is that verse from Zephaniah."

Her father had never been a terribly expressive man, especially about his faith. It was almost as if he wanted to be a counterpoint to Aunt Becca's bold speech.

To hear him speak like this, not in logical statements but in this tender voice, quoting Scripture, made tears spring to her eyes. "It doesn't feel like He's with me, Dad."

"When has faith ever been about feelings?"

That silenced her, both her mouth and her spirit.

Because she realized that for much of her life, her faith *had* been about feelings.

Pressure to attend church with her family.

Guilt if she didn't do what her Sunday School teachers said she should do.

Longing to please her father and Aunt Becca, to be a good daughter.

Had she ever really come to God on her own terms? Just herself? Without her family in the background?

And why did she only realize this now, when her heart was broken and she didn't want to come to God, when she felt completely abandoned by the God she'd grown up knowing?

But she had to admit, here she was, not going to Him because she didn't *feel* like it. Wasn't that again putting her feelings before her faith?

Did God want her faith despite her feelings? Or along with her feelings of betrayal and abandonment?

The Lord your God is with you, He is mighty to save.

Zephaniah 3:17. A Sunday School memory verse from years ago.

She closed her eyes. *You already know how I feel. But maybe You truly are with me. Maybe You are mighty to save.*

Paltry words. *But, God, that's the best I can do now. I will choose to try to believe You.*

And maybe, hopefully, that was all He wanted from her.

"Dad, I found them." Rachel's voice broke her reverie as she entered the living room, carrying a box of papers.

Her father's face lightened as he caught sight of the box. "Excellent."

"Found what?"

"When you called to tell us about the office being ransacked and the background checks being gone, I had Rachel start looking for some old files I'd kept in my office." He pulled out a manila folder. "I thought I'd made copies of the background checks, but I wasn't sure if I still had them."

"Copies?" She reached for a folder.

"I don't know if I have the most recent staff additions, however. But these should be most of them."

This was the best news she'd heard all day.

Something to do. Something to keep her busy. Something that might help.

Devon dreamed of Naomi.

She had turned into a statue, and water was streaming out of an urn in her hands into the basin of a fountain. She turned blank eyes to him and opened her mouth, but only ringing came out of it. She opened and closed her lips, and each time, a shrill ringing would sound for a second before she closed her mouth.

"What is it? What are you trying to tell me?" he asked her.

Ring, she replied.

Actually, it sounded a lot like a telephone…

Devon cracked an eye open and saw only darkness. Then a piercing sounded through the hotel room, jolting his heartbeat. He fumbled with the phone on the nightstand. "Hello?"

"Devon, it's Martha."

"What is it? What time is it?"

"It's three o'clock in the morning. Devon, there's been a fire."

"What?" Suddenly he was wide awake. He sat up in bed and reached for the lamp.

"Two fires, actually. Someone broke the lock on the storage shed in your backyard and set fire to everything inside."

"There wasn't much in there. Nothing valuable."

"But then they broke the window to your spare bedroom—the one filled with boxes—your other storage room."

Oh, no. In that room, he stored tax forms, a fire-resistant safe filled with cash and valuables, and some special family mementos. "They broke into the house? What about the alarm?"

"They broke the window and set off the alarm, but they didn't enter the house. They sprayed gasoline into the room and set fire to it."

"No. Oh, no."

"Luckily, your neighbor's son—Reggie Velasquez—was sneaking into his house after staying out too late, and he saw the fire. He called the firemen immediately, so it didn't spread beyond the storage shed and that room."

Talk about coincidence. Reggie was a quiet, straight-A student—this was the first Devon had heard about him sneaking out. What were the odds?

"God was watching over your house, Devon, because it could have been so much worse."

"I know." Yes, it could have been worse.

And maybe God was watching over him, too.

"The Velasquezes had my number as your emergency contact, so they gave that to the police, and they called me."

"I'm sorry they had to wake you, Martha. This is above and beyond the duties of an admin."

"I don't mind because my boss is going to give me a very nice Christmas bonus," she replied tartly. "Are you driving back here soon?"

"I'll leave in a few minutes." He tossed off the covers and searched for his shoes.

"I'm going to tell my husband and then drive to your house. I'll meet you there."

"Thanks, Martha." He hung up the telephone.

He grabbed his cell—three missed calls. All Martha, all about five minutes ago. He must not have heard it ring, so she had called the hotel instead.

3:13 a.m. It was late, but he had to tell Naomi where he was going. Maybe, like himself, she wouldn't hear her cell phone so he could just leave a message. He dialed.

She picked up on the second ring. "Hi, Devon."

She sounded surprisingly alert for three in the morning. "I'm sorry, did I wake you?"

"No, actually. Dad found copies of the background checks for the spa staff, so I was looking through them."

"Copies? That's great. But at this hour?"

He could almost see her give a one-shoulder shrug. "I couldn't sleep. What's up?"

"There's been a fire at my home."

"What? Oh, no."

"No one was hurt, my neighbor's kid saw the fire in time. And it was just in one room of the house."

"Thank God." It was a prayer, not an expletive.

He felt the same way.

"I'm heading back to Atherton right now."

"Drive carefully. How far away is your home? I don't really know where Atherton is."

"I live south of my office in South San Francisco. About two hours away." He slipped his laptop into the case.

"Oh." Silence.

"Are you okay?"

"It's nothing. You just live…farther away from Sonoma than I realized." Her voice was small, although he could tell she was trying for a light tone.

"Naomi." He set down his laptop bag. "When this is over, we'll talk. And if…" He looked at the Gideon Bible he'd been thumbing through just before bed, which still sat on the bedside table. "If God wants us to be together, then it'll work out. We'll make it work out."

Now the silence was laced with shock. Finally, she said, "I never thought I'd hear you say that."

"People change." He picked up his laptop bag again. "I'll call you later. Stay safe—don't take any risks. You've got that bookie after you and the murderer is still around."

"Yes, sir."

"Naomi…" *I love you.* "Get some rest."

"I love you, too." She hung up.

He stared at his cell phone. Was he dreaming? Had she said what he thought she said? Had he spoken aloud without realizing it?

Despite the worry over the fire, despite his hurry to drive back home, something sweet unfurled in his chest, something beautiful and powerful and glorious.

The drive to Atherton was long and tedious, but free of traffic since it was so late—or early, depending on how he looked at it.

He arrived two hours later. The fire trucks had already left, but water still dripped from the eaves of his home. Sticky heat wrapped around him as he got out of his car.

The next thing that wrapped around him was Martha, hugging him fiercely. "I'm so thankful you were in Sonoma and not in that house."

So was he. The acrid smell of smoke and ash seemed to clog his throat, layer in his lungs.

Martha released him. He bent to kiss her cheek gratefully. "Only one room was burned?"

She nodded. "And the storage shed. The fireman I talked to said it was obviously arson, unless you make a habit of keeping gasoline in your storage shed and your back bedroom."

"After everything that's happened, I'm almost not surprised it's escalated this way." He had kept her informed about the events in Sonoma, since he was still away from work. He just couldn't go back to his normal routine while Naomi was in so much danger. "Can I go in back?"

"I don't think so. There's a fire official around here somewhere. He'll want to talk to you."

"Are they sure it's arson?"

"Can't you smell the gasoline? I heard one of the firemen say it looked like whoever set the fire splashed gasoline everywhere outside, but the blaze didn't grow large enough to catch it on fire."

The next few hours were a blur. Devon spoke to an arson investigator about what had happened, where he'd been, when he could schedule a walk-through.

He spoke to his neighbors. He thanked Reggie Velasquez, although Mr. Velasquez was still giving his son a hard eye that promised retribution later for the reason his son had been able to call the fire department in the first place.

They looked with curiosity at the cut over his eye from the car accident, but didn't mention it. Thankfully, he hadn't fulfilled Monica's dire prediction and didn't have a black eye, and most of his other injuries weren't visible.

Martha stayed with him the entire time, silent but supportive. It was almost as if she didn't want to leave him, for fear that something would happen to him if she did. Maybe she wasn't too far off base with those sentiments.

Late in the morning, he stood in front of his house, which looked like normal from this angle. If he went to the Velasquezes' yard and got up on tiptoe, he could see over the side fence and catch sight of the blackened roof of the metal storage shed in the backyard.

Why the shed? What had he had in there? Some gardening tools, his old mountain bike…and boxes belonging to Jessica. Lots of boxes of her belongings.

Most of them had been things like clothes or old magazines. But there had also been a few boxes of knickknacks, mementos, pictures.

Was this the connection, then, between her murder and the attacks against him? Was he being targeted because of Jessica? Had she been killed for some obscure reason rather than her stolen necklace? Was the murderer now after him because of his old connection with her?

What could he know about Jessica that was worth killing him for?

SEVENTEEN

Naomi fell asleep over the background checks, and woke up just as the sun cascaded through her window into her bedroom. But it wasn't the sun that had awakened her—it was Aunt Becca's strident voice.

"You can't go back there."

"I don't see why not." Rachel sounded patient and reasonable, but Naomi caught the undercurrent of irritation in her placid voice.

"It's not safe. There's a murderer on the loose."

"It's perfectly safe. The lab is probably one of the safest places in Sonoma because of the card key entrance and the security guards on duty. And the outside video surveillance."

"You heard Naomi—the murderer is one of the spa staff."

"The solution is simple. I'll enter the lab and tell the security guards to reprogram the card key entrance not to let anyone else in."

"So you'll be all by yourself in the lab?"

"I'll be locked in, protected by the card key doors and the security guards."

"Why do you need to go in to work so soon? Can't it wait?"

"Aunt Becca." Now Rachel's voice had a definite annoyed edge to it. "I need to work on my research. We have a new project launch already scheduled. I can't put off my experiments any longer." Her voice started to move away. "Besides, Naomi and Devon are the ones targeted, not me."

Naomi jumped up from the floor, rubbing the cheek that had been pressed against the background checks when she'd fallen asleep. She flung open her bedroom door. "Rachel."

"What?" came from the bottom of the stairs.

Naomi hurried around the corner to the landing and down the stairs. "Has Gloria Reynolds tried to talk to you recently?"

Rachel paused in slinging her purse over her shoulder. "No. But why would she want to speak to me?"

"I think she knows about your research."

Rachel grew very still. Her eyes widened slowly as she stared at Naomi. "That's impossible."

"When I went to talk to her, she mentioned having the family over to dinner, and more importantly, she wanted to get better acquainted with you. Why would she target you if she didn't know about your research with diamond powder?"

Rachel worked her bottom lip with her teeth. "It didn't even work very well."

"It doesn't matter. How did she know about it?"

"Do you think it's connected to the murders somehow?"

Naomi shrugged helplessly. "We know the murderer is a staff member. But not everything makes sense. Maybe this thing with Gloria is completely separate. Maybe everything is completely separate."

"I don't know about Gloria, but I do think Devon

Knightley's accidents are connected to Jessica Ortiz somehow." Rachel picked up her keys from the basket in the hallway.

"But there's no proof."

"If we wait long enough, we'll probably get proof."

"If we wait long enough, Devon might be dead."

Rachel's face fell. "Oh. That's true." She opened the front door. "Well, I'll be at the lab," she said, then left.

How like Rachel to say something like that, and then abruptly leave. Some days Naomi couldn't believe they were related.

She headed back upstairs to change. She wondered how Devon was doing, how his house was.

I love you, too.

She squeezed her eyes shut at the memory. Had she really said that to him? It was just that when he'd hesitated, she heard the words *I love you* almost as clearly as if he'd spoken them. And the response had just popped out of her mouth. Maybe she'd been tired and not thinking clearly.

Except she had meant it.

She wasn't sure how things would work out with them. He lived and worked so far away from Sonoma, and for now, her life was here—running the spa while her father recovered, and then being groomed to take over later…

Except she was only managing the spa out of a sense of obligation. Because she wanted to please her dad, to fulfill family expectations. But she'd known for months that it wasn't what she wanted to do.

But who else could do it?

Was she again doing something based on feelings—in this case, guilt and a desire to please—rather than what God wanted? Was this just like her shaky faith?

She had other things to think about for now.

As she and Aunt Becca ate breakfast, they looked over the background checks.

"Here it says James worked in a car garage for a while," her aunt said, reviewing a folder.

"So?"

"So, he might have known how to tamper with Devon's brakes."

"But the driver who tried to run him down was a woman."

"Oh. Well."

"How about Kallie?" Naomi asked.

"What about her?"

"Jessica always asked for Kallie for her facials."

"But on this visit, she had an appointment with Haley for the day after she was killed," Becca said.

"She did? I wonder why?"

"Remember the last time Jessica was here? Kallie was going through a rough time—she was taking care of her mother."

"That's right. She was distracted at work. And then her mom died."

"She seems almost okay now. She knew her mom was near the end, so she wasn't unprepared."

"And it's been four months since she died." Naomi flipped to another paper—and stopped. "Do you remember when Sarah was hired?" she asked.

Aunt Becca frowned as she thought. "April?"

"This background check is dated April. But the last time Jessica came into the spa was March—before Kallie's mother had passed away."

"And?"

Naomi put down her fork, because it was trembling. "How did Sarah know Jessica Ortiz liked to talk? Or that Jessica liked to come in early before her appointments?"

"What are you talking about?"

"Sarah, Iona and Haley came into my office after Jessica died. They were the ones who suggested I talk to the other Tamarind members who might have spoken to Jessica. I remember Sarah saying to me, 'Do you know how Ms. Ortiz likes to talk?' Or something like that." Naomi could picture Sarah's face in her mind as she suggested that Naomi speak to the Tamarind members. Her eyes had been wide and excited that the girls had come up with something that might be useful. All three of the girls had been talking, but she definitely remembered one of them saying the idea had been Sarah's.

Naomi pointed to the background check. "She was hired after Jessica's last visit. How would she know Jessica liked to talk?"

"Maybe Iona or Haley told her."

"Haley never had Jessica as a client. She always asked for Kallie. And Sarah spoke as if she knew Jessica."

"Did she know Jessica from before she came to work for us?" Aunt Becca asked. "Could that be possible?"

"But she never said anything about it."

"Maybe she forgot?"

"Well, where did she grow up? Here it is. Glory, Californ—" That name was familiar, partly because it was so unusual. Where had she heard that town before?

"Glory. Glory. Where did I hear that town lately?"

Devon. She vaguely recalled hearing his voice say the name of the town. Why would he tell her about Glory, California? Why would he mention it?

"Jessica's from Glory! That's the connection!" She jumped up and raced upstairs to get her cell phone. She dialed Devon just as her aunt followed her into the room.

"Hello, beautiful."

Even with her heart pounding with a mix of fear and apprehension, the endearment made her smile. Thank goodness she hadn't put the call on speakerphone yet. She did so now. "Devon, Aunt Becca's here with me. She and I just discovered something. Did Jessica ever mention knowing Sarah?"

"Sarah who?"

"My receptionist, Sarah Daniels."

"Um…"

"The one who was just engaged to a very wealthy boyfriend," Aunt Becca supplied.

"Oh, yes, I remember. The one with the gigantic diamond engagement ring. No, Jessica didn't mention someone named Sarah. How did she know her?"

"From her hometown—Glory, California," Naomi said.

"Jessica didn't often talk about her friends from Glory. She lost touch with them after her parents moved the family to San Francisco."

"How about the yearbook?" Naomi said.

Aunt Becca shook her head. "Sarah is in her mid-twenties and Jessica was around thirty-five. They wouldn't have gone to high school at the same time."

"The yearbook!" Devon's voice crackled on the speakerphone. "Naomi, that's why someone set fire to my storage shed."

"What?"

"The arsonist torched my storage shed and the back bedroom, which I was using as storage. The storage shed had boxes of Jessica's things, all labeled with her name. The arsonist could have easily seen them just by looking inside the shed—it has a small window."

"The murderer was trying to get rid of some type of evidence," Aunt Becca said.

Naomi thought back to when Devon brought the box to the spa. "Do you remember, Aunt Becca, when you and some of the staff looked at the box of Jessica's things before Devon showed it to me? Was Sarah there?"

"Yes."

"It must be the yearbook, Devon. And it's gone," Naomi said.

"No, it's not."

"But the fire—"

"I never got around to putting the box back in the storage shed. I forgot. It's still in my car trunk."

The world stopped turning for a brief moment. Then she took a gasping breath. "Devon."

"I'm opening the trunk now." The sound of the trunk popping open. Pages ruffling. Then silence.

"Devon?"

"Naomi, I'm going to send a few pictures to you."

"Devon, what's wrong?"

"Just take a look at the pictures. I can't be sure…"

"Sure of what?"

Her phone blipped as she received the pictures he'd taken with his phone. Her aunt crowded next to her to see. She pressed a few buttons—and stared at a complete stranger.

"Who is that?" she said.

"That's Sarah Daniels from Jessica's yearbook," Devon replied.

It took a moment to sink in. This stranger was Sarah Daniels.

The real Sarah Daniels.

"Devon." Her voice came rushing out of her throat, raspy and sharp. *"Who is the woman I've been calling Sarah Daniels?"*

"And what happened to this Sarah Daniels?" Aunt Becca exclaimed.

Suddenly, pieces fell into place. "Jessica recognized her. The false Sarah. Knew who she really was."

"She killed Jessica before she could expose her," Devon said.

"Why kill Eloise?" her aunt asked. "And why take the necklaces?"

"We talked about that," Devon replied. "The necklaces were inconsequential. The real need was to get rid of Jessica. I don't know why she killed Eloise Fischer, though. Did Eloise come from Glory, too?"

"No, Eloise didn't even really know Jessica." Naomi thought back to her conversation with Eloise. "She knew Jessica's mother."

"Maybe Jessica's mother knew about the real Sarah, or the false Sarah," her aunt said.

"I think she's the 'Andrea' Jessica mentioned when she died," Naomi said.

"How would Sarah—or rather, Andrea—know that Eloise Fischer was acquainted with Jessica's mother?" Devon asked.

Naomi remembered Iona walking into the Anise Lounge with a tray of wineglasses. "Iona. Eloise mentioned Jessica's mother when Iona was in the room with us. Andrea must have asked Iona what we talked about and found out that Eloise knew Jessica's family."

"And killed her in case Eloise knew too much."

"Poor Eloise," Aunt Becca whispered. "I doubt she knew anything at all."

"But Andrea made a mistake," Devon said. "She thought Naomi was at lunch when she killed Eloise, but Naomi was with a last-minute client and had an alibi."

"That must have really upset her." Naomi shivered. "Andrea had obviously planned everything carefully— right after she found out Eloise knew Jessica's family, she stole my credit card number to pay for the lamp."

"And she planted the napkin on Eloise, not knowing it was my blood and not yours," Devon said.

"But Devon, why would Andrea try to kill you?" her aunt said. "She tried to run you down even before you found the yearbook."

"Maybe she was afraid of what I knew about Jessica's past. After all, she knew I was Jessica's ex-husband."

"Now it makes sense," Naomi said. "She wanted to frame me, so she tried to break into my car but couldn't—she only mangled the lock. But she knew Marissa Paige had the same make and model car. She followed them to the restaurant. Managed to steal the keys out of Marissa's purse. Drove to your hotel. Laid in wait for you."

"Except she didn't know you and Becca would be walking by when it happened," Devon added.

"She's dangerous."

"We need to tell Detective Carter."

"We don't have proof. We need to show him that yearbook."

"I'm on my way," Devon said, starting his car engine.

"Hurry." She ended the call.

"You call Detective Carter," her aunt said as she left the room. "I'll go clean up the kitchen and get the background checks for you to give to the detective later."

Naomi called the detective, but he barked, "Yes?" when he picked up the phone. There was a lot of noise and bustle in the background.

"Detective Carter, this is Naomi—"

"I know, Miss Grant. What do you need?" Someone nearby him shouted, but she couldn't make out the words.

"I think that my receptionist, Sarah Daniels, is the murderer." It sounded awful, saying it aloud.

"Why?"

"I think she's not really Sarah Daniels. I think she's Andrea—the 'Andrea' that Jessica Ortiz mentioned before she died."

"How do you know this?" More voices in the background. Things sounded stressful and frantic.

"She's from the same hometown as Jessica Ortiz, but the picture of Sarah Daniels in Jessica's yearbook is a different person from the woman I know as Sarah."

"Where's the yearbook?"

"Devon Knightley is driving to Sonoma with it. Can we come by the station—"

"No, do not come by the station. We have a situation here right now. I'll come find you when I'm done."

"Oh." What was going on? she wondered. Things sounded very serious. "Okay. I'm at home."

"I'll talk to you later, Miss Grant."

Before he hung up, someone spoke to the detective. "The bomb squad is ready, sir…"

Bomb squad? There was a bomb threat at the station?

The fire at Devon's house. The bomb threat at the station. Was all this Andrea's work?

That was silly. Andrea couldn't be everywhere at once.

But maybe this meant she was about to do something. Something bad.

Naomi gripped the edges of her desk, forcing herself to breathe deeply. She was safe here. Her father, her sister Monica and Aunt Becca were here with her. All she had to do was stay put at the house and not do anything stupid.

"Naomi!"

She went to the stair landing and saw her aunt in the foyer, poking through her purse for something. "Naomi, did you call Detective Carter?"

"I just did." She summarized their brief conversation.

"Good. Stay here," Aunt Becca said, fishing her keys out of her purse.

"Where are you going?"

"I have to go to the spa. Rachel called my cell phone from the lab. She could hear my office phone ringing almost constantly for the past hour."

"Why?"

"I just checked my voice mail. Moya Hillman's manager left twenty messages—she forgot her meds in her locker and needs them. I'm going to let the manager into the spa to get them." Aunt Becca strung her purse over her shoulder.

"Be careful."

"I'll be fine. I'll also be able to check up on Rachel."

Naomi didn't want her aunt to leave her. But that was silly. Dad and Monica were in the house.

"I'll be right back. It won't take me more than forty-five minutes to get there and back."

While Naomi waited for Aunt Becca to return, she went online to research Sarah Daniels and Glory, California. But she didn't find anything. The name alone was too common to give her manageable results.

So she tried Jessica Ortiz and Glory, California. That got a few targeted hits. Jessica had won a few school awards, and a few newspaper articles about her father's business mentioned her hometown.

Jessica had been homecoming queen in her senior year. The newspaper picture showed a smiling young woman with a wide, bubbly smile, sitting on a papier mâché throne with a cheap tiara on her head. Students crowded around her—the picture had been taken at the homecoming game, apparently.

And in a small corner of the photo, there was Andrea.

She was much younger, but with the same lovely eyes, pert nose and rosebud mouth. She looked like she was about ten years old. She looked dazedly at the camera as if unaware that she was in the picture of Jessica.

I got you.

After this picture was taken, Jessica and her family had moved to San Francisco because her father expanded his business. What had happened to Andrea? How long had she stayed in Glory until she moved here to Sonoma?

And what happened to the real Sarah Daniels?

Where was Detective Carter's business card? It had his e-mail address so she could send him this picture. She looked through her purse, then started sorting through her desk drawers. Her cell phone rang.

Caller ID said it was Iona. Why would she be calling? "Hello?"

"Miss Grant." Iona spoke in a shaking whisper. "Please help me."

Her entire body tensed. Iona and Sarah were friends outside of work. "What is it? Where are you?"

"I'm in Sarah's apartment. I'm in her bathroom. Oh, Miss Grant." She swallowed a sob. "I was looking for toilet paper. I looked under her sink…and Miss Grant, *Ms. Fischer's ruby pendant is there.*" Iona's soft sobs carried over the line.

"Iona, calm down."

"Please help me. I don't know what to do. Miss Grant, what do I do?" Panic threaded through her whispered words.

Naomi started to shake, too, but she grabbed her purse. "Stay in the bathroom. Pretend you're sick. I'll get the police and come to Sarah's apartment."

"Please hurry." Iona clicked off.

Naomi called Aunt Becca. "Yes, dear?"

"Iona's in Sarah's apartment. She found Eloise's pendant under the bathroom sink and she's scared out of her mind."

"I'm not yet at the spa. Don't you dare go to Sarah's apartment alone."

"I'm not going to. Can I meet you at the spa?"

"Yes. Did you call the detective?"

"I'm going to do it right now."

"Good girl. I'll meet you at the spa."

Naomi got Sarah's home address from the staff directory and hurried to Dad's room, but stopped at the threshold at the sight of Monica and her father glaring at each other. "Dad?" Why did they have to choose this moment to have another fight?

Monica glanced her way, then turned and stalked past her out of the room. Dad took a thin breath through flaring nostrils, then said in a tight voice, "Yes?"

"I'm…going to the spa to meet Aunt Becca." She'd explain later. She had so much to explain anyway—she realized that she'd never told him about what she'd just discovered about Sarah/Andrea.

"Fine."

She called Detective Carter as she headed out the door to the garage. It went straight to voice mail. "Detective Carter, this is Naomi Grant. My other receptionist Iona is at Sarah Daniels's—not the real Sarah, the false Sarah's apartment—and she just found Eloise Fischer's necklace there. She's scared and she called me. I'm going to the spa to meet my aunt Becca. Please call me back as soon as you can."

She slipped her cell phone in her pocket, so she'd have quick access in case he called her back when she was driving.

Naomi and Aunt Becca would wait at the spa until they could go to Sarah's apartment with the police. Assuming Detective Carter let them follow. She hoped he would, if they promised to stay at a safe distance. She wanted to be there for Iona. What a thing to discover about her best friend.

She got into her car as the garage door slid open. As she started the engine, she heard a click. That was strange. She looked in her rearview mirror—

Right into the eyes of Andrea.

EIGHTEEN

"Don't move."

Something cold and metallic pressed against her neck.

Naomi couldn't speak. Couldn't breathe. Her heart was racing so fast, it was going to explode in her chest.

"Back out of the garage."

Her hands wouldn't respond. Her feet were welded to the floor.

The gun pressed harder into her neck. "Do it."

She couldn't shift gears. Her hand shook so much, she kept missing Reverse.

Andrea knocked the tip of the gun into Naomi's jaw, hard.

She flinched. The car went into Reverse.

"Drive to the highway."

She complied, her entire body sensitive to the motion of the car, every bump and jerk.

She found her voice. "Iona…"

"She's fine. I just used her phone. Hard to tell someone's voice when they're whispering, isn't it?"

Naomi hadn't even suspected.

Should she let Andrea know everything? Would it make her desperate, or would it make her abandon her plan if she knew too many people had already pieced things together? What would she do if she knew Devon was on his way back to Sonoma with the yearbook that she'd failed to destroy?

"You weren't surprised when you saw me," Andrea remarked.

A pang went through Naomi. She hadn't stuttered in surprise to see her receptionist in her backseat holding a gun.

"It doesn't matter if you have figured it out already. You won't live much longer."

Naomi gripped the steering wheel tight to keep herself from screaming.

They turned onto the winding two-lane highway. Could she cause a car accident? Would that enable her to run away?

"Hand me your cell phone."

Naomi stopped herself just in time from reaching in her pants pocket. *Her broken cell phone was in her purse.*

Blood pounded in her ears as she rummaged in her purse and pulled out the broken phone. Would Andrea look closely at it, see that it was broken?

No, she didn't even glance at it before sliding a window down and tossing it out of the car.

Thank You, God.

"Pull over here."

She stopped on the side of the stretch of road. Would someone pass by? Naomi wondered. Could she scream? Was anyone close enough to hear her?

"Pop the trunk and get out of the car."

She watched the gun barrel as she obeyed. It never wavered.

"Get in the trunk."

She bent to climb in, noting that Andrea had removed her roadside emergency kit and the tire iron from the trunk. No hope of a weapon.

Then pain crashed into the back of her head.

Devon was about half an hour from Sonoma when he received Becca's frantic phone call. "Have you seen Naomi?"

"I'm driving up to Sonoma now."

"She's not answering her cell phone."

Something sharp twisted in his gut. "Maybe she can't hear it in the house."

"I called Augustus. She left an hour ago to meet me at the spa. She's not here."

"Why was she going to meet you at the spa?"

"Iona called from inside Sarah's apartment. She had found Eloise Fischer's necklace under the bathroom sink and was frightened. Naomi said she'd call the police and meet me at the spa."

"Did she call the police?"

"Detective Carter said he got a voice mail from her about it, but when he called her back, she didn't pick up. He hasn't heard from her since."

Panic clawed at his insides like a wild tiger. "I'll meet you at the spa, Becca."

"Please hurry."

Oh, God. Oh, God. He didn't know what to pray. He didn't want to voice his fears.

His tires squealed as he turned into the spa parking lot. Becca ran up to his car. "She set Naomi up."

"Andrea?"

"I got a call from a client's manager who needed to get into the spa to get her meds, but she never showed up. Detective Carter says they received a false bomb threat at the station—he received a package that was nothing but putty and wires."

"Where's the detective?" Devon asked.

"At the station." Becca got into his car. "He's waiting for us. Do you have the yearbook?"

"Yes."

As they headed out Becca's cell phone rang. "Hello? Oh, hello, Carlos..." She suddenly sat up. "What? When?"

He couldn't keep his eyes on the road. He glanced at her.

Her hand was over her mouth as she listened. "And you're sure it was her car?"

Naomi's car? He strained to hear, but all he caught was the tone of Carlos's voice, tinny as it sounded through the cell phone.

"We'll be right there." She closed the phone. "Go back to your hotel."

"What did Carlos see?" He looked for a place he could turn around.

"He says he saw a woman he didn't recognize driving Naomi's car past his restaurant. She parked at your hotel, went inside, then came right back out again and drove off."

"He's sure it was Naomi's car?"

"Yes. He's obsessed with cars. He remembered the Paiges' license plate number."

"So what does he think the woman did?"

"He doesn't know, but what *I* think is that she left you a message."

He stepped on the gas.

Sure enough, slipped under his hotel room door was another note. This one had been printed on a laser printer, however.

Dear Devon,
I can't live the lie any longer. My gambling addic-
tion has taken over my life. Even the necklaces will
not bring me enough to pay back what I owe. I hope
you can forgive me.
Naomi

"What?" He read it again.

Becca bit her lip as she read over his shoulder. "Remember, this isn't Naomi. That's what Carlos said."

Suddenly Devon remembered the call from the bookie, and the pieces slid into place with echoing finality. "She's set Naomi up to take the fall for the murders. Andrea incurred gambling debts by posing as Naomi, and reneged on paying them. There's a dangerous bookie after her."

"What?" Becca stared at him in horror. "When? And why didn't you tell us?"

"I told Naomi." Obviously she hadn't told Becca, probably so her aunt wouldn't worry more.

"So Andrea took the necklaces—"

"As a ruse to make people think Naomi killed those women for their jewels, in order to pay off her gambling debts."

Becca stared at the letter again. "No one would believe it of her. This letter is too heavy-handed."

"What are the police going to believe? Assertions without proof or a letter?"

Becca's face turned pasty. "Or not a letter. Maybe stronger proof."

"What do you mean?"

"Devon." She grabbed at his arms. "What if she intends to kill Naomi? With Naomi dead—and maybe the neck-laces found on her—the case is closed." Becca gripped his hands and closed her eyes. "Father God, please protect Naomi—"

Protect her? When was He going to start protecting her? He snatched his hands out of hers. "I can't. Becca, I can't pray."

Her eyes were startled and wet with tears. "You can. You have to."

"No, I don't." There was a chasm between them, huge and yet small at the same time. "He's...He's..." He couldn't voice it.

"He's here."

"He's never been here! Where is He?" His breath came in gasps. Naomi was in danger. "I can't pray to Him."

Sparks flew from her eyes. "Well, then, what are you going to do?"

"What?"

"I have something to do, someone to trust in. Who do you have to trust in? Have you just given up?"

"No!"

"Well then, *what are you going to believe?*"

He couldn't answer. He took in her trembling lips, her rapid pulse, the red splotches on her clammy cheeks. "So are you telling me He's going to answer my prayer just because I believe in a crisis moment?"

"No."

He blinked.

"He just wants you to believe, even if He doesn't answer us. Devon, He wants you to believe, period. Not just because you suddenly need him."

"How would I know the difference?"

"You don't have to. He will."

That's why He was God.

And Naomi had no one else right now.

He had no one else right now.

Becca must have seen his emotions on his face, because she clasped his limp hands in hers and held on tight. "Our dear Jesus, please protect our girl."

Her cell phone shrilled. She reached into her purse and checked caller ID.

"It's Naomi."

NINETEEN

Naomi woke slowly. She groaned as she moved…except she couldn't move. Her wrists were bound tightly, but a folded cloth protected her wrists from abrasions from the zip ties. That didn't make sense. Her ankles were also zip-tied together, and the cloth of her pants was bunched under the plastic.

Blood pounded painfully behind her eyes. She shut them.

Oh, God. God, please help me.

The Lord your God is with you, He is mighty to save.

Was He really? Would He really?

"It doesn't feel like He's with me, Dad."

"When has faith ever been about feelings?"

She bit back a sob. *Oh Lord, I need You now.*

The Lord your God is with you, He is mighty to save.

Suddenly, the car slowed down. She didn't have much time.

She fumbled in her pants pocket. Her cell phone was still there. She pressed buttons frantically, dialing Aunt Becca's speed-dial number and turning the phone on speakerphone. She shoved the phone back in her pocket and hoped Andrea wouldn't notice its bulge.

The trunk opened, and sunlight sliced through her eyes. She struck out blindly, but her hand only glanced off a shoulder.

Andrea yanked her from the trunk. Naomi teetered on her tied feet, then fell to the ground.

Gravel bit into her cheek, her hands, filled her nose. She coughed as it coated her throat. Her head throbbed, fueled by the bright light and the pain in her limbs.

She squinted as she looked around. They were in a sheltered turnoff. A remote stretch of highway, with rolling foothills rising to one side. Scraggly trees lined the edge of the turnoff.

"Where are we?"

"Don't recognize it?" Andrea had gotten a rusty nail out of the backseat.

"A road to Napa? Trinity Road?"

Andrea didn't answer. Naomi hoped her aunt was listening, and hoped her guess had been right. There were a handful of roads between Napa and Sonoma.

Andrea unearthed a hammer from the backseat and proceeded to pound the rusty nail into the front tire.

"What are you doing?" Naomi sat up. Her head protested with a few throbs that felt like hammer blows to the back of her head.

Andrea took out Naomi's jack and lifted up the front of the car. It took her a long time because she wasn't strong, and the work was awkward for her.

Watching her, Naomi realized that even though she was bound, she was still stronger than Andrea. Years of performing massages had honed her upper body strength and torso.

If she had a chance, she'd have to take it. Gun or not.

With Andrea distracted, Naomi twisted her wrists. Too tight. She twisted her ankles.

The cloth of her pants slid with her movements.

Slowly, she pulled her pants legs out from under the zip tie. The bond was looser. She loosened her shoes.

Andrea finally hoisted the car up, except she positioned the jack badly. The car wasn't stable. It swayed dangerously as it rose higher and higher.

Andrea unscrewed the lug nuts of the punctured tire. Again, it took her a while because of her weak arm strength and her nails.

Take as long as you like.

Andrea rolled the lug nuts out of the way. Then she casually rolled one lug nut under the car, near where the jack hiked it up.

She spoke, sounding positively cheerful. "And that's to explain why you're under the car in the first place."

"What…what do you mean?"

"When they find you crushed under the car," Andrea replied calmly. "The jack will have fallen over while you reached under the car for the lug nut."

"You won't get me under that car."

"Yes, I will." Andrea picked up the tire iron. "No one will notice another bump on your head once it's been crushed by the car."

That's why there was a cloth protecting her wrists from the marks of the zip tie, and why Andrea had tied Naomi's ankles over her pants legs. So there wouldn't be evidence that Naomi had been bound when her body was found.

"Why are you doing this?" she shouted. "What have I ever done to you?"

"Nothing much, really." Andrea dropped the tire iron and pulled a bag out of the backseat of the car. "Although I was upset at you for a while when my fiancé first met you."

"Why?"

For the first time, Andrea's calm eyes blazed with an inner fire. "Because I could tell he was attracted to you. It took a great deal to get his mind off you and back on me again. For a while, I wasn't certain I could get him to propose because of how he'd responded to you."

"But I barely spoke to him." Naomi couldn't even recall the man's face. He'd stopped in one day at the spa to see Andrea, and Naomi had said barely ten words to him. He hadn't impressed her—he was the pompous type who liked his women submissive, and Naomi wasn't submissive by a long shot.

"It doesn't matter, really, because he eventually did propose. But don't you see? Jessica would have messed everything up."

"Messed what up?" Naomi had to keep Andrea talking.

"Do you know how long it took for me to find a man with money? How long it took to get him to propose?" Andrea reached into the bag and diamonds glittered like stars. Jessica's necklace. Then she pulled out Eloise's ruby pendant.

She tossed them into the backseat.

"Why did you take those?"

"No, *you* took those. To pay off your gambling debts."

"Gambling?" Then she remembered the phone call. The ten thousand dollars. "I don't gamble."

"Of course not. I gambled for you." Andrea reached into the bag and pulled out some sheets of paper. "These won't mean much to you, but the police will know what they are." She tossed those into the backseat, too.

No.

Like a caged animal, Naomi felt the rage and panic build up within her. She wouldn't be taken. She wouldn't be trapped. "They know you're not Sarah Daniels. I told the police."

"Do you have proof? Concrete proof?" Andrea stared down at her with eyes cold as a snake's. "What do you have that proves I'm not Sarah Daniels? Sarah has been corresponding with her friends from Glory, California, for years. She sent birthday presents to her widowed mother until she died, and paid the mortgage on her house."

The headache was making it hard for Naomi to focus. "You paid another woman's mortgage?"

She shrugged. "It wasn't much. Real estate in Glory is a joke. But it bought me something else." She smiled. "Credibility."

Andrea picked up the tire iron again.

"Wait. You'll get blood on it." A desperate plea.

"No. I've got bleach—"

Naomi swung out with her legs and swept Andrea's feet out from under her. The tire iron sailed through the air and landed a couple feet away.

Naomi needed time. She shot her legs out and landed a solid blow to Andrea's jaw.

"Oomph!"

Andrea rolled to the side, hands going to her face.

Naomi kicked off her shoes and tugged the zip tie off her ankles. Even without the fabric of her pants legs, it was a tight fit. She shoved frantically, and the plastic sliced into her skin. The blood made it easier for it to slide off.

The gravel chomped on her bare feet as she stood. Andrea was reaching for the tire iron.

Naomi kicked it aside, the metal colliding painfully with her bare foot as the gravel slid away in a cloud.

Andrea scrambled up and lunged for the tire iron.

Naomi lunged after her, and landed on top of her.

Andrea squirmed and clawed. Naomi landed a blow with her elbow against Andrea's side. It only made her thrash harder.

Naomi hoisted her torso up a few inches and wrapped her arms around Andrea's neck, her wrists still bound.

She twisted left, trying to hook her right elbow under Andrea's chin. Andrea dropped her head, keeping her from getting a good grip. They struggled—Andrea tried to curl up, Naomi tried to slide the crook of her elbow under her throat.

Gravel and dirt burned Naomi's elbow. Sweat dripped down her arm, making it hard to keep a tight hold of Andrea.

She bunched up her shoulder muscles and crunched them hard.

Her elbow slid past Andrea's chin, right against her esophagus.

Naomi squeezed for all she was worth.

Andrea's lower body bucked against her. Naomi almost lost her grip. She clenched her stomach tight so she could press her choke hold harder.

Andrea's arms came up, plucked at Naomi's hair, shoulders. Then she got a sharp blow into Naomi's eye.

Pain exploded. Naomi's eye watered. She squeezed her eyes shut, ducked her head, and held on.

Andrea's movements slowed. Her blows became more feeble.

She stopped moving as Naomi heard the distant wail of sirens.

Devon followed the last police vehicle dangerously close with Becca in his passenger seat. Detective Carter had taken Becca's phone, but she clutched her hands to her chest as if she were still cradling it.

The cars pulled off to the side of the road in a cloud of dust. Devon yanked on the steering wheel and skidded to a halt. Becca was out of the vehicle before it had stopped.

They saw Naomi's car, its right front end hoisted up.

Beyond it, two women on the ground.

Detective Carter helped the topmost woman to her feet. *Naomi.* Devon ran to her.

She fell into his embrace with a sob.

He felt her entire body trembling. He held her closer.

"Devon." Sweet. The sound was sweet.

He pulled back slightly, then bent to kiss her, hard.

She was laughing and crying when he lifted his head. Her hair was tangled around her face, and she had scratches along her cheeks. But she was alive. She was alive.

"Don't ever leave me," she said.

"I'll never let you go."

TWENTY

It was now or never.

"Naomi, grab the Chinese chicken salad and take it out to the patio." Aunt Becca bustled past her with a tray of sushi, while the buzz of their guests sounded through the open patio doors.

She'd been trying to talk to her father for days now. While he was profoundly glad that she was all right, he and Monica still hadn't returned to calmer footing in their relationship, which made him moody.

Monica wouldn't say what they'd argued about, but Naomi worried that it was the usual—Monica's firm desire not to live in Sonoma, not to help with the family's spa. And her father's stubborn insistence on family loyalty, family commitment, family support.

Naomi didn't want to talk to him.

But she had to.

She'd promised Devon she would.

Dad seemed in a more cheerful mood today, maybe because of the small party they were giving for lunch. This was the first social gathering he'd had since his stroke, and it made him feel less like an invalid to have people around him.

Detective Carter had been invited. They'd discovered that the detective had tried to put off arresting Naomi for as long as he could, and he had tried to smooth her way through the system.

Naomi still didn't think he had "kind eyes," but Aunt Becca had forgiven him, if her coy behavior was any indication.

Devon's family had arrived a few minutes earlier and were waiting on the patio. Her father was still in his bedroom, about to come down. Naomi had convinced Monica to let her help him instead of herself.

"Take him," Monica had said, fire still smoldering behind her eyes. "He's still not talking to me."

"Dad?" Naomi entered his bedroom. He sat on his bed, fully dressed.

"Ready to go down?" Excitement tinged his voice.

"Before we do, I need to talk to you, Dad." She stood stiff and straight, her neck stretched out, hoping his disappointment wouldn't hack her head off.

His face was neutral.

"Dad, I'm happy to take over things at the spa while you're recovering, but once you're okay, you'll need to train someone else to eventually inherit the spa."

There. She'd said it.

His eyes grew stormy. "What? Why? You're the only one I trust to take over." Underlying his words was his bitter disappointment at Monica's insistence on having nothing to do with the spa. At least Rachel's all-consuming dedication to her research kept the spa popular with her exclusive skin care products.

Naomi felt her jaw quivering. She had to do this. "Dad, I've been praying about it."

"Praying about what?" he asked impatiently.

"Taking over the spa isn't what I want to do."

"Taking over the spa is your duty as my daughter."

Honor your father and mother. "Dad, I'm managing things now. But you're getting better every day. You're still young. You'll be in charge of the spa for many years."

"Naomi." His voice and his eyes were heavy. "I had a stroke. Life is short."

"Which is why I want to make sure I'm spending my life doing what I feel God wants me to do. And it's not running the spa. I'm sorry."

He turned his face away. Naomi couldn't tell what he was feeling.

"Dad, you can find someone else and train them."

"I wanted one of my daughters to take over."

"Do you remember you told me, 'When has faith ever been about feelings?' Dad, despite what you want, can't you trust that God will provide the right person to manage the spa for you?"

It was a bold thing to say, especially to her father. But despite the trembling running through her stiff frame, she felt a peace that told her she was doing the right thing.

"This sudden decision is because of Devon Knightley."

"No, it's not." It was only partly because of him. "It's because everything that's happened to me in the past week and a half has forced me to acknowledge that 'The Lord your God is with you, He is mighty to save.' I had to believe in Him despite my fear, and He saved me."

Unspoken was what she wanted him to understand— that her dad had to believe in Him despite his fears for the spa and his health, and He would save them all.

The silence ticked by. She let her father process what she'd been saying. She wished she could see his face, but it was probably for the best.

Finally, he sighed and turned to look at her. She couldn't tell what he was thinking.

"Do you love Devon?"

"Yes, Dad."

"Then…I suppose that's what's important."

A concession.

But she also knew her father would pray about it.

"Come on, Dad. Let's join our guests."

Naomi liked Devon's sister, Rayna. She was more bubbly than her brother, but apparently very fond of him.

His parents were a different story, although his mother seemed to respect her, and his father felt sorry for all that had happened to her.

Sitting next to him on the Grant family's back patio, the two of them looked like trauma unit victims—Naomi bandaged up from her fight with Andrea, Devon moving stiffly from his numerous bruises.

"We're quite a pair, aren't we?" He reached for her hand.

"I hope this isn't indicative of the rest of our relationship."

"You're bad luck," he teased.

Eventually, the general chitchat turned to what was on everyone's mind.

"Detective, did Andrea finally confess? And what's her real name?" Naomi asked.

He hesitated before answering. "Her real name is Andrea Mulvany. She was the real Sarah Daniels's neighbor. Andrea hasn't confessed, but we've pieced things together. Sarah Daniels was working in Glory when she disappeared a few years ago, around the time Andrea left to work in the Bay Area. We think she killed Sarah then, although the Glory police are now looking for her body."

Naomi's throat closed over the sip of green tea she'd just drunk.

"People thought Sarah was still alive because her friends received e-mails from her a few days after she'd disappeared. Sarah said she'd decided to move to San José to find a better job so she could pay off her mother's mortgage."

Andrea had told Naomi that. She had paid off the mortgage for Sarah's mother. Had pretended to be a daughter to a woman not even related to her. "What about Andrea's real family?"

"She apparently had argued with them about moving, so she severed her ties entirely. They hadn't heard about her until we spoke to them a few days ago."

What a shocker, to find out that their daughter had been living another woman's life. "So she took Sarah Daniels's identity? Why?"

"We're not sure. Sarah's family had stable finances, whereas Andrea's family was very poor. Sarah had a rather normal family life, whereas Andrea's home life was very turbulent." The detective shrugged. "Who knows what kind of psychological forces would make a woman kill another and take her identity?"

"And no one said anything when Sarah just up and left?"

"We don't know what Andrea said to Sarah's mother when Sarah disappeared. Publicly, at least, Sarah's mother seemed to be pleased and supportive when her daughter unexpectedly left. She died a few years later from a heart attack, so we'll never know."

"Well," Aunt Becca said as she lifted her head. "I pray Andrea eventually finds peace in Christ."

Devon's father turned red and looked like he was about to say something, but Mrs. Knightley put a firm hand on his arm. Aunt Becca smiled sweetly at him.

"Family gatherings are going to be very interesting," Devon whispered to Naomi.

"Family gatherings?" Naomi looked at him, her heart beating a rapid tap-tap-tap. "Your family and my family? That's assuming our families have a reason to get together." Like a marriage.

His hand, holding her left one, loosened enough for him to rub a thumb over her bare third finger. "Don't play coy, Miss Grant. You know very well we'll have a reason."

Devon's eyes thrilled her. She'd kiss him if her father weren't standing a few feet away, trying not to glare at their twined hands.

He brought her fingers to his lips, pressed a soft kiss on her knuckles. "I never want to leave you, Naomi. I want the right to protect you and love you."

Her hand tingled. "What if I want to protect you?" From pain like what Jessica inflicted on him. From fear of being alone.

"God will protect us both."

And then, despite his father and her father, despite the other avid eyes around them, he reached over to cup her jaw and leaned in to kiss her.

* * * * *

Dear Reader,

I have loved taking on a romantic, suspenseful journey through the beautiful agricultural county of Sonoma, California. The first time I visited Sonoma, I knew I needed to set a book there, and where better to plan mayhem and murder than in a tourist hotspot that still has that small-town feel? Sonoma is also very rich in history as well as in breathtaking views of the countryside.

Naomi's story was fun to write because I see so much of myself in her strong personality. (I also give a pretty good massage!) Her struggles with her faith—based on feelings—are especially dear to me because they're what I struggled with when I was right out of college. I had been a Christian for a few years, but I realized I needed a deeper, truer relationship with God.

Naomi's theme is a special one for me, because it reminds me that God really is in control no matter how crazy things become. Like Naomi, I don't always trust or feel that God is with me, but He always manages to come through for me despite that. I am hoping many of you will relate to her struggles just as I do.

I love to hear from readers! You can e-mail me at camy@camytang.com or write to me at P.O. Box 23143, San José, CA 95123-3143. I am very prolific on my blog, http://camys-loft.blogspot.com/ and I invite you all to join me there, if only to see my mental state of the day.

Camy
Tang

QUESTIONS FOR DISCUSSION

1. Naomi is trying to be a good manager of the spa, which sometimes means saying no to clients with politeness and courtesy. In the opening scene, she doesn't do a very good job and her aunt Becca has to step in. Have you ever been in a situation where you had to tell someone no politely? How well did you do? How did it make you feel?

2. Devon is still recovering emotionally from a bitter divorce. Can you relate to his anger and struggle to forgive? Have you had a hard time forgiving someone who hurt or betrayed you?

3. Aunt Becca is a strong Christian who is also very outspoken about her faith. Can you relate to her or do you know someone like her? What is your own way of sharing your faith?

4. Naomi's staff are friends who hang out with each other outside of work. Do you have a close relationship with your coworkers? Is there someone you might want to get to know better at work?

5. When Naomi realizes someone is trying to set her up for the murders, she feels helpless and stressed. Have you been in a situation where things were completely out of your control and it seemed to be going from bad to worse? How did you feel? What did you do?

6. Naomi is struggling with the reality that someone she knew has died, even though Jessica wasn't a close

friend or a family member. Have you had a coworker, classmate or friend pass away? How did it make you feel? How did you cope with the loss?

7. Devon has a poor relationship with his parents, and Naomi's warm family circle draws him in. Why is it important to have people—either family or like family—around you? Do you have a "family" circle of your own?

8. As things get worse, Naomi knows she needs to trust God and believe that He's got everything under His control, but she has a hard time doing this. Instead, she takes charge to try to do something about the murders and the person framing her. Have you ever felt this way? How did you respond? What would you have done differently from Naomi?

9. After the phone call from the racetrack bookie, Naomi feels God has forsaken her. Have you ever felt that way? How did you respond? Did you have people to pray with you or talk with you?

10. Devon is falling in love with Naomi and wants to rescue her from the insidious net closing in around her, but there's nothing he can do. Have you ever wanted to rescue someone but were too helpless to do anything?

11. Naomi's father mentions that faith is not about feelings. For Naomi, it means she's only been going through the motions of faith for most of her life because her family is Christian. Can you relate to

that? Or can you relate to trusting more in your feelings than your faith?

12. Naomi's theme verse is Zephaniah 3:17: "The Lord your God is with you, He is mighty to save." What does that verse mean for you?

Dumped via certified letter days before her wedding, Haley Scott sees her dreams of happily ever after crushed. But could it turn out to be the best thing that's ever happened to her?

Turn the page for a sneak preview of
AN UNEXPECTED MATCH
by Dana Corbit,
book 1 in the new
WEDDING BELLS BLESSINGS *trilogy,*
available beginning August 2009
from Love Inspired®.

"Is there a Haley Scott here?"

Haley glanced through the storm door at the package carrier before opening the latch and letting in some of the frigid March wind.

"That's me, but not for long."

The blank stare the man gave her as he stood on the porch of her mother's new house only made Haley smile. In fifty-one hours and twenty-nine minutes, her name would be changing. Her life as well, but she couldn't allow herself to think about that now.

She wouldn't attribute her sudden shiver to anything but the cold, either. Not with a bridal fitting to endure, embossed napkins to pick up and a caterer to call. Too many details, too little time and certainly no time for her to entertain her silly cold feet.

"Then this is for you."

Practiced at this procedure after two days back in her Markston, Indiana, hometown, Haley reached out both arms to accept a bridal gift, but the carrier turned and deposited an overnight letter package in just one of her hands. Haley stared down at the Michigan return address of her fiancé, Tom Jeffries.

"Strange way to send a wedding present," she murmured.

The man grunted and shoved an electronic signature device at her, waiting until she scrawled her name.

As soon as she closed the door, Haley returned to the

living room and yanked the tab on the paperboard. From it, she withdrew a single sheet of folded notebook paper.

Something inside her suggested that she should sit down to read it, so she lowered herself into a floral side chair. Hesitating, she glanced at the far wall where wedding gifts in pastel-colored paper were stacked, then she unfolded the note. Her stomach tightened as she read each handwritten word.

"Best? He signed it *best?"* Her voice cracked as the paper fluttered to the floor. She was sure she should be sobbing or collapsing in a heap, but she felt only numb as she stared down at the offending piece of paper.

The letter that had changed everything.

"Best what?" Trina Scott asked as she padded into the room with fuzzy striped socks on her feet. "Sweetie?"

Haley lifted her gaze to meet her mother's and could see concern etched between her carefully tweezed brows.

"What's the matter?" Trina shot a glance toward the foyer, her chin-length brown hair swinging past her ear as she did it. "Did I just hear someone at the door?"

Haley tilted her head to indicate the sheet of paper on the floor. "It's from Tom. He called off the wedding."

"What? Why?" Trina began, but then brushed her hand through the air twice as if to erase the question. "That's not the most important thing right now, is it?"

Haley stared at her mother. A little pity wouldn't have been out of place here. Instead of offering any, Trina snapped up the letter and began to read. When she finished, she sat on the cream-colored sofa opposite Haley's chair.

"I don't approve of his methods." She shook the letter to emphasize her point. "And I always thought the boy didn't have enough good sense to come out of the rain, but I have to agree with him on this one. You two aren't right for each other."

Haley couldn't believe her ears. Okay, Tom wouldn't have been the partner Trina Scott would have chosen for her youngest daughter if Trina's grand matchmaking scheme hadn't gone belly-up. Still, Haley hadn't realized how strongly her mother disapproved of her choice.

"No sense being upset about my opinion now," Trina told her. "I kept praying that you'd make the right decision, but I guess Tom made it for you. Now we have to get busy. There are a lot of calls to make. I'll call Amy." Trina dug the cell phone from her purse and hit one of the speed dial numbers.

Haley winced. In any situation, it shouldn't have surprised her that her mother's first reaction was to phone her best friend, but Trina had more than knee-jerk reasons to make this call. Not only had Amy Warren been asked to join them downtown this afternoon for Haley's final bridal fitting, but she also was scheduled to make the wedding cake at her bakery, Amy's Elite Treats.

Haley asked herself again why she'd agreed to plan the wedding in her hometown. Now her humiliation would double as she shared it with family friends. One in particular.

"May I speak to Amy?" Trina began as someone answered the line. "Oh, Matthew, is that you?"

That's the one. Haley squeezed her eyes shut.

* * * * *

*Will her former crush be the one
to mend Haley's broken heart?
Find out in AN UNEXPECTED MATCH,
available in August 2009
only from Love Inspired®.*

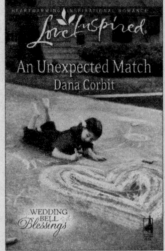

REQUEST YOUR FREE BOOKS!
2 FREE RIVETING INSPIRATIONAL NOVELS
PLUS 2 FREE MYSTERY GIFTS

Love Inspired®
SUSPENSE

YES! Please send me 2 FREE Love Inspired® Suspense novels and my 2 FREE mystery gifts (gifts are worth about $10). After receiving them, if I don't wish to receive any more books, I can return the shipping statement marked "cancel". If I don't cancel, I will receive 4 brand-new novels every month and be billed just $4.24 per book in the U.S. or $4.74 per book in Canada. That's a savings of over 20% off the cover price. It's quite a bargain! Shipping and handling is just 50¢ per book.* I understand that accepting the 2 free books and gifts places me under no obligation to buy anything. I can always return a shipment and cancel at any time. Even if I never buy another book, the two free books and gifts are mine to keep forever.

123 IDN EYM2 323 IDN EYNE

Name	(PLEASE PRINT)	
Address		Apt. #
City	State/Prov.	Zip/Postal Code

Signature (if under 18, a parent or guardian must sign)

Mail to Steeple Hill Reader Service:
IN U.S.A.: P.O. Box 1867, Buffalo, NY 14240-1867
IN CANADA: P.O. Box 609, Fort Erie, Ontario L2A 5X3

Not valid to current subscribers of Love Inspired Suspense books.

Want to try two free books from another series?
Call 1-800-873-8635 or visit www.morefreebooks.com

* Terms and prices subject to change without notice. Prices do not include applicable taxes. Sales tax applicable in N.Y. Canadian residents will be charged applicable provincial taxes and GST. Offer not valid in Quebec. This offer is limited to one order per household. All orders subject to approval. Credit or debit balances in a customer's account(s) may be offset by any other outstanding balance owed by or to the customer. Please allow 4 to 6 weeks for delivery. Offer available while quantities last.

Your Privacy: Steeple Hill Books is committed to protecting your privacy. Our Privacy Policy is available online at www.SteepleHill.com or upon request from the Reader Service. From time to time we make our lists of customers available to reputable third parties who may have a product or service of interest to you. If you would prefer we not share your name and address, please check here. ☐

LISUS09

Love Inspired SUSPENSE

TITLES AVAILABLE NEXT MONTH

Available August 11, 2009

SPEED TRAP by Patricia Davids

The fatal crash was no accident. The only mistake was leaving behind a four-month-old survivor. For the boy's sake, Sheriff Mandy Scott *will* see justice served. Yet Mandy finds herself oddly drawn to her prime suspect—the boy's father, Garrett Bowen. If Mandy trusts Garrett, will he shield her from danger, or send her racing into another lethal trap?

FUGITIVE FAMILY by Pamela Tracy

Framed for murder, Alexander Cooke and his daughter fled to start a new life. A life that brings Alex, now Greg Bond, to charming schoolteacher Lisa Jacoby. Then the true killer returns. This time, Alex can't run. Because now he's found a love—a family—he'll face anything to protect.

MOVING TARGET by Stephanie Newton

A dead man on her coffee shop floor. An ex-boyfriend on the case. Sailor Conyers has murder and mayhem knocking at her door. She'll need her unwavering faith and the protection of a man from her past to keep her from becoming the killer's next target.

FINAL WARNING by Sandra Robbins

"Let's play a game..." Those words herald disaster as radio show host C. J. Tanner is dragged into a madman's game. Only by solving his riddles can she stop the murders. And only Mitch Harmon, her ex-fiancé, can help her put an end to the killer's plans.

LISCNMBPA0709